THE MOVIE
Junior Novelization

THE MOVIE
Junior Novelization

Adapted by Kate Howard from the script by T. J. Fixman,
Gerry Swallow, and Kevin Munroe
Based on characters created by Insomniac Games

SCHOLASTIC INC.

© 2016 Sony Computer Entertainment America LLC. Ratchet & Clank characters © Sony Computer Entertainment America LLC. Ratchet & Clank movie © 2015 Ratchet Productions, LLC.

Published by Scholastic Inc., *Publishers since 1920*. SCHOLASTIC and associated logos are trademarks and/or registered trademarks of Scholastic Inc.

The publisher does not have any control over and does not assume any responsibility for author or third-party websites or their content.

This book is a work of fiction. Names, characters, places, and incidents are either the product of the author's imagination or are used fictitiously, and any resemblance to actual persons, living or dead, business establishments, events, or locales is entirely coincidental.

ISBN 978-1-338-03041-9

12 11 10 9 8 7 6 5 4 3 2 1   16 17 18 19 20

Printed in the U.S.A.   40
First printing 2016

Prologue

ABOVE THE PEACEFUL PLANET TENEMULE, Alonzo Drek towered over his minions. Chairman Drek was the commander of a powerful space station called the Deplanetizer and the leader of the Blarg, an alien species with big green eyes and pointy teeth.

"Esteemed citizens of Quartu," Drek called to his gathered troops. "I stand before you a proud Blarg!" Drek's meaty jowls quivered as he made his way along a bridge walkway on a motorized scooter. "Tonight, we will twist the very fabric of reality. We will defy nature with reckless abandon!"

Drek's robot assistant, Zed, zoomed along the space station's bridge behind the chairman. Zed hovered behind Drek. He was always ready and willing to do his master's bidding.

"We have also broken sixteen galactic statutes and one star ordinance . . . ," the evil leader continued. Drek shook a finger at his troops. "So I shouldn't see anything about this online!"

A dozen Blarg snapped their phones shut, cowering under their commander's watchful gaze.

Drek cleared his throat, letting his eyes wander over the crowd below him. "In just a few moments, we will unleash a weapon so powerful that it will take—" Drek stopped suddenly, for one of his minions was typing away on his phone. "Stanley, are you seriously *still* texting after what I just said?"

Stanley squeezed in a few last-second keystrokes and then slammed his communicator closed. He smiled up at Drek sheepishly.

Drek's eyes narrowed. He knew just how to take care of problems like this. "Victor?" he called out, gesturing toward Stanley. "If you please . . ."

A door whooshed open, and Drek's first lieutenant stepped out of the shadows. Victor Von Ion was an enormous silver instrument of destruction—more than five times the size of a Blarg.

Stanley cowered in fear as Victor thundered toward him, ready for action. Victor's arm swooped down, and his metallic fingers wrapped around Stanley's head. He lifted the frightened Blarg up and dangled him in midair.

"Mommy!" Stanley whimpered.

Victor continued to squeeze the disobedient Blarg until, suddenly, Stanley's phone announced, "Dialing mother."

While Stanley dangled face-to-face with Victor, his phone began ringing. A moment later, Stanley's mother's voice squeaked through the speaker, "Hello, Hunkleberg residence! Hello?"

Victor held out his hand, wiggling his enormous fingers. Stanley dropped the phone into the robot's hand. Victor tossed it into his mouth and chewed.

Metal crunched between Victor's teeth, and Stanley's mother's voice screeched, "Who is this?"

Victor swallowed the phone, his message delivered. Then he dropped Stanley back to the floor.

Drek smirked. "Now, does anyone *else* feel like texting? Show of hands." He scanned the room. "Anyone?"

One Blarg began to raise his hand, but his neighbor pulled it down before Drek could see.

"Very well . . . ," Chairman Drek boomed. "Commence deplanetization!"

"Ready the Deplanetizer!" a Blarg lieutenant shouted.

With a mighty roar, the Deplanetizing machine came to life. The entire space station rumbled as six giant targeting arms blazed with power. The central core glowed, ready to destroy anything in its path.

The lasers focused on the planet Tenemule. An instant later, a beam of white energy blasted out of the weapon's core.

Boom! The planet glowed white for a moment before exploding into dozens of pieces. The Blarg cheered as the chunks of the destroyed planet of Tenemule scattered throughout the galaxy.

CHAPTER ONE

ON THE DESERT PLANET OF VELDIN, music was pumping from somewhere near the Kyzil Plateau. "498 . . . 499 . . . 500!" the punishing voice of a fitness instructor growled from a TV screen.

In front of the TV, a lone Lombax named Ratchet did push-ups as a pumped-up Solana trooper led his morning workout.

"Is that all you got?" the trooper's voice boomed from the TV. "Come on now. No pain, no gain! One and two and three and four. If you can feel the burn, that's good! If you can smell the burn, that's bad."

Ratchet grunted and huffed, struggling through his workout. Though he was exhausted, he was intense and focused. He staggered around his loft, trying to keep up with the demanding exercise regimen.

Ratchet glanced up at the posters of the Galactic Rangers plastered all over the walls of his home. Maybe they would inspire him through the rest of the video. *Come on*, he thought as he ran in place along with the Rangercise program. *If you want to be a Ranger, you've got to be tough!*

"Okay, let's dig deep," the Solana trooper commanded. "Don't quit on me now. Can you feel it? Can you feel the burn?"

"Are you kidding?" Ratchet huffed. "I'm on fire! I can take anything you can dish out, so bring it on!"

The Solana trooper dropped to the floor and began doing one-armed push-ups. "Okay," he said, not the least bit out of breath. "Two thousand more!"

"Two . . . thousand?" Ratchet squeezed in a single push-up, and then collapsed.

"No pain, no gain!" the trooper reminded him. "*Ranger Workout* will be right back after these messages."

Ratchet flicked through the channels, happy for a short break. His small frame was definitely burning. He wanted to be a Ranger, but their workouts were insane! He stopped flicking channels, settling on a news channel just long enough to hear the newscaster say, "Planet Tenemule is no more!"

Ratchet gaped at the screen. "What?"

"Hello. Dallas Wannamaker here," the newscaster went on. "Tonight at five, another uninhabited planet is destroyed without warning or cause, marking the fourth in recent memory in our once-peaceful galaxy. As a result, the president has requested that our ever-vigilant Galactic Rangers increase their numbers . . . from four to five."

Ratchet scooted closer to the TV as a shot of his four heroes flashed across the screen. *The Galactic Rangers!* "And now, a message from the man himself: Captain Qwark!" Dallas Wannamaker continued.

The TV went black, and then a shot of Ratchet's lifelong role model filled the screen. Captain Qwark's muscles rippled beneath his green superhero suit. "Space!" he boomed. "A wondrous realm full of adventure and peril and, uh . . ." Qwark stuttered for a moment, searching for a word that would sound powerful. "Um, and er . . . *bigness.*"

"Captain Qwark!" Ranger gasped.

"The Solana Galaxy is our home," Qwark went on. "As many of you know, it's in a state of crisis. The Galactic Rangers are looking for a new recruit to help with the investigation." On-screen, Qwark bent down and put his arm around a tiny kid. "So if you're a small-time nobody in search of adventure, come on down to the spaceport and see me—Captain Qwark!"

Ratchet watched as the screen filled with shots of the four Rangers in action—Qwark, Cora, Brax, and Elaris. They were amazing! Of course, Ratchet had followed his heroes closely since he was a tiny Lombax. He'd seen all their best moves before. But it never got old. He loved watching the Rangers do their thing.

"Our next stop," Qwark's voice rang out, "Planet Veldin's Kyzil Plateau!"

Ratchet's eyes went wide with joyous disbelief. That's where *he* lived! "Kyzil Plateau?!"

"That's right," Qwark said. "The Kyzil Plateau!"

"Ranger tryouts!" Ratchet said, leaping to his feet. "This

is huge!" He jumped onto his foldout bed and began firing away at invisible assailants with his remote control.

"Galactic Ranger," he cried in his toughest voice, spinning to shoot at the air. "Grab some sky!" He pivoted left and then flipped into the air. The bed wobbled. "Watch it, punk. I'm a highly trained—"

Suddenly, the bed slammed closed, trapping Ratchet inside.

"Ranger down . . . ," Ratchet whimpered.

"Hello?" a voice called out from the repair shop below. Ratchet could hear the service bell ringing. It was one of his customers, Mr. Micron.

"Helloooo? I'm here to pick up my ship," Mr. Micron called.

Ratchet pressed against his bed with all his might, but it wouldn't budge. It popped open just a crack and then squeezed his fingers when it slammed shut again.

Ratchet had a feeling none of the Galactic Rangers ever got trapped in their own beds. Sighing, he called out, "I'll be there in a sec."

CHAPTER TWO

WHEN RATCHET FINALLY MADE IT DOWN to the shop, Mr. Micron was shuffling his walker slowly across the giant garage. Ratchet couldn't wait to show the old dude his all-new, fixed-up ship. He pressed a button and the simple spaceship rose up on the shop's electric lift.

Grinning, Ratchet turned on some music and called out over the PA system, "Are you ready to have your mind blown?"

"Uh . . . no?" Mr. Micron wheezed. He shuffled past his ship, which was now spinning in the air over his head.

Ratchet activated his swingshot, a gadget on his wrist that let him shoot a long rope that latched onto faraway objects. He used it to swing through the air, landing right in front of Mr. Micron. "I'll take *that* as a yes!" He hit another button, and the little ship began to transform. Mr. Micron looked on, stunned, as his simple spaceship morphed into a souped-up starship.

"Boom!" Ratchet said.

Mr. Micron's mouth hung open.

Ratchet quickly pointed out all the new features he'd installed on the ratty old ship. "Protolux afterburners . . . full Gadgetron weapon package . . . and a high-intensity Mag-Booster so powerful it can pick up a paper clip from two kilocubits away!"

Mr. Micron shuffled forward, unimpressed. "I think there's been a mistake. I came in to get my ejector seat repaired."

Ratchet grinned. "Why *repair* something when you can *improve* it? Come on, have a seat." He waved Mr. Micron toward the ship, urging him to climb into his new vehicle. When the old guy didn't move, Ratchet reached down and gave him a boost.

Reluctantly, the elderly Tharpod settled into the pilot's seat. Ratchet leaned over the side of the ship door, showing off his hard work. He had put a lot of time into Mr.

Micron's ship, and he was proud of what he'd created. He loved fixing up ships and turning them into something way fiercer than anyone could have ever imagined.

"Now," Ratchet said, pointing to a switch. "Let's fire up that Mag-Booster!"

Mr. Micron's shaking finger flipped the switch. The ship hummed, and then—

Clang! A screwdriver flew across the shop and clung to the magnetized ship.

Mr. Micron shrieked. Ratchet waggled his eyebrows. "Pretty sweet, right?"

"I guess," murmured Mr. Micron. "But why do I need it?"

"Well, you could . . ." Ratchet scratched his big ears, thinking about his customer's question. "I mean, you know, if you ever, uh . . ." He chewed his lip. Mr. Micron really wasn't in the market for a fabulous fighting machine. "Y'know, I don't know."

Suddenly, a wrench flew across the room and embedded itself inches from Mr. Micron in the pilot's seat. The old guy screamed again.

"Whoa!" Ratchet said, cringing. "No worries, I can buff that scratch out. Maybe we should just power this sucker down . . ." He reached into the ship and tried to flip the switch to OFF—but it was busted. "Oh boy."

Ratchet leaped out of the way as another tool pinged the ship right beside him, and then another, and another. In an instant, every piece of metal in the garage was pulled toward the magnetized ship.

Ratchet and Mr. Micron both ducked as metal flew at them from all sides.

"Look out!" Ratchet cried. "Watch it!"

A Qwark action figure flew through the room and stuck to the ship. "You're going down like a lead balloon, pal," the toy squeaked.

"Hey!" Ratchet said. "I've been looking for that."

As Ratchet dodged and weaved to avoid the incoming metal, his tail accidentally flicked against a switch on the ship's control panel. The afterburners roared to life.

"Wh-what was that sound?" Mr. Micron said, spinning nervously in his seat.

"Nothing," Ratchet lied. After a beat, he added, "Unrelated question: Is your seat belt on?"

A moment later, the ship blasted out of the garage at full speed. A hurricane of tools careened after them.

Ratchet clung to the side as Mr. Micron steered around obstacles. Both screamed as the ship zoomed toward Kyzil Canyon.

"Hit the brakes!" Ratchet yelled. "Hit the brakes!"

Mr. Micron pressed blindly at pedals. He hit the wrong one, and the ship rocketed forward even faster.

Ratchet was tossed to the back of the ship like a rag doll. "Those aren't the brakes!" he screamed, clinging to the ship.

"I'm too old to die. Ahhh!" Mr. Micron cried.

"You've got to be kidding me," Ratchet said, rolling his eyes. "How did you get a license?"

As the ship bounced and lurched through the canyon's walls, Ratchet yelled out, "Can you hit the kill switch, please?"

"The fish witch?" Mr. Micron yelped.

"The *kill switch*! On the dash!"

Mr. Micron stared at the dash, overwhelmed by the sheer number of buttons and switches. He flipped them at random, hoping luck would be on his side. But nothing happened.

"Hang on," Ratchet called. "I can fix this." Using his swingshot, he launched himself back into the pilot's seat. He dove onto the floor and opened a control panel.

Mr. Micron batted at Ratchet's tail. "Your tail's in my face," he moaned.

"Hey, the view's no prettier down here, pal," Ratchet grunted. He extracted a mess of wires from the panel as the ship ricocheted off a wall and careened around a corner into a narrow canyon.

Mr. Micron screamed. "There's a wall!"

"Ooh boy," Ratchet said, holding up two wires. He twisted them together. "Yes!" he cheered.

Seconds before the ship crashed, Ratchet pressed the brakes again. The ship skidded, screeching to a halt a hairbreadth from disaster. All the assorted metal tools that had been trailing behind them flew past and exploded against the dusty canyon wall.

"Phew!" Ratchet said, grinning. "That was a close one, huh?"

Mr. Micron gaped at him. A moment later, the ejector seat launched the old guy high into the sky. "I want a refunnnnnnnd!" he screamed.

Ratchet cringed. "Yeah, I have a feeling that's gonna show up on my midyear review . . ."

On the planet Quartu, a layer of smog hung thick and black over the headquarters of Drek Industries. Factory chimneys belched out clouds of pollution over the dismal Skorg City skyline.

"You seem especially brooding today, Victor," Drek told his enormous robot bodyguard. "Come! I have just the thing to brighten your day!"

Drek sped into his office on his scooter. He gleefully pointed to a hologram of the beautiful and serene planet Novalis in the center of the room. "Our next target. Look at these waterfalls. The fjords! The rolling hills of Corvoxian Snodgrass! This is exactly what I need." He pressed a button, and images of Novalis's most scenic landscapes filled the room. Drek spun in happy circles, nearly dancing with glee.

"But, sir," Victor grunted. "That entire region is heavily patrolled by the Galactic Rangers."

"We *will* have this planet," Drek went on, ignoring Victor. "And we will take it by going on the offensive. Our forces will strike at the Galactic Rangers first and remove them from the equation altogether!"

Victor was slightly cheered at this piece of news. "Wait . . . *real* battle?"

"Metal hand against hand," Drek promised. "I trust this pleases you?"

"Of course it pleases me," Victor growled. "But we don't *have* any forces."

Drek waved away his concern. "You let me worry about that. Soon the Galactic Rangers will be destroyed, and I'll be able to complete my masterpiece!"

CHAPTER THREE

WHEN RATCHET RETURNED TO THE GARAGE with Mr. Micron's ship, his boss was waiting for him.

"How many times, Ratchet?" Grimroth Razz asked. The burly, tusked Fongoid shook his head, irritated. "How many?"

Ratchet parked the ship, and then shrugged. "Come on, he's fine. He landed in a pile of ivy."

"*Poison* ivy," Grim grunted. "Look, you're my best mechanic, and you've got a lot of heart. But you're careless."

"'Careless' is such an ugly word," Ratchet said, tapping a wrench against his palm. "I prefer 'carefree.'"

Grim glared at him. Ratchet held up his hands. "Too soon? Yeah, it was too soon."

Grim looked up from the ship he was repairing. "Listen, I know things haven't been easy for you, but you can't keep acting out like this when I have a shop to run. What's with you lately?"

Ratchet sighed. "I just feel like I'm supposed to do more. I've always dreamed of being a Galactic Ranger, doing big things—like Captain Qwark!" He held up his Qwark trading card, wiggling it in front of Grim's face.

Grim was unimpressed. "You want an old Fongoid's advice? Dream smaller. It leads to less disappointment."

"Please, Grim," Ratchet pleaded. "I just need one hour off so I can go to the spaceport for tryouts."

Grim shook his head. "You promised you'd help me give proton scrubs to every ship on the plateau! It's almost summer—these people depend on us!"

"First off," Ratchet said, undeterred, "it's *always* summer. We live in a desert. And second, that promise is still in effect. It's a one hundred percent valid promise, and you can redeem it . . . in one hour." Ratchet looked at Grim with pleading eyes.

Grim took a deep breath, and then sighed.

"Yes!" Ratchet whooped, pumping his fist. "You! You are a great friend, Grim. Don't let anyone tell you different." He hopped onto his rocket sled and blasted out of the garage. "I'll be back before you know it!"

As Ratchet flew away, he called back, "You're the best boss in the galaxy. An inspiration to us all. Don't ever change!"

The Kyzil Fairground was bustling with Galactic Ranger hopefuls. Hundreds of residents had turned up to try to convince Captain Qwark they had what it took to be the fifth Galactic Ranger.

Ratchet raced through the crowds toward an enormous stage, eager for a front-row seat. He had never seen the Rangers live and in person before!

"Ladies and gentlemen," an announcer called from backstage. "Get on your feet. Put your hands together and give a big planet Veldin welcome to your . . ." A glowing orb rose out of the center of the stage. Music pumped through the crowd. ". . . Galactic Rangers!"

The orb opened, and a tall, slim alien holding two huge guns came racing out. "First up," called the announcer. "She'll shoot first and ask questions when she's good and ready . . . Cora Veralux!"

As Ratchet watched in delight, the announcer continued, "Next up: You loved him in Grapplemania, you love him as a Galactic Ranger . . . get ready to feel the pain of Brax 'the Brute' Lectrus!"

Brax jet-packed into the sky, and then zoomed down and over the crowd before landing dramatically on the main stage.

"And finally, he's a legend in his own space and time, ladies and gentlemen. The savior of Solana, Captain Qwark!"

Qwark rose out of the orb, which blazed with fire. Qwark stepped through the flames, flexing his muscles and showing off his physique for the crowd.

"Hello, Veldin!" Qwark called.

"Hello, Captain!" Ratchet and all the other fans chorused back.

"As you know," Qwark told the crowd, "my name is Copernicus Qwark and, yes, that was an impressive wall of fire I just walked through." Qwark stopped and posed, waiting for the oohs and ahhs.

"He's on fire again," Brax muttered to Cora from the edge of the stage.

"I know," Cora said, rolling her eyes. She stepped forward and blasted Qwark with a fire extinguisher.

Qwark didn't seem to notice he'd been on fire—or that he'd been doused with foam. He struck a new pose. "I'm going to be real with you folks for a moment. When President Phyronix recommended I take on a new Ranger, I knew just where to go. That's right . . . we want you!" He pointed at the crowd. Ratchet cheered along with the rest of Veldin's hopefuls.

"The galaxy is a perilous place. Invasion. Space pirates. *Supernovas!*" Qwark continued. "I know what you're thinking: Do I have what it takes? After all, you may not have prevented Dr. Nefarious from atomizing Aleero City."

Qwark preened in front of a giant monitor that showed images of his greatest conquests. The crowd went wild.

"You may not have stopped Neftin Prog from rendering the entire population of Cortox City color-blind . . . twice!"

The crowd oohed.

Qwark rubbed his chin and lowered his voice, transfixing the crowd with his charm. "You may not have this chiseled jaw or godlike pectoral region. But if you have heart, then you have what it takes."

Ratchet's eyes went wide with hope. He *did* have heart! He couldn't wait to show Captain Qwark just how *much* heart.

But when his turn came to meet with the Rangers for his interview, Qwark was unimpressed. "You don't have what it takes," the captain told him.

Ratchet's ears fell. He was devastated. "But . . . I have heart."

"Yes," Qwark said flippantly. "But unfortunately, that heart is encased in a weak, muscleless mass of inexperience. Plus, there's your history to consider."

The other Rangers flipped open their tablets and scanned Ratchet's file. Ratchet slumped in his seat as they studied him.

"Got a long line of citations here," Cora said, gazing down at him. "Possession of an illegal Gravity Repulsor?"

"That was a misunderstanding!" Ratchet insisted. "I thought that space pirate was on the level."

Brax fixed him with a steely gaze. "Operation of a black-market accelerator?"

"'Operation' is a strong word," Ratchet argued. "It blew up as soon as I turned it on!"

"Willful disruption of the space-time continuum?" Cora gasped, scanning through the file.

"*That*," said Ratchet, "is a funny story."

"You're reckless," Qwark said, slamming his huge fists onto the table. "You're a loose cannon. And you're dangerous." He glared at Ratchet. "That's *my* shtick."

Qwark ushered Ratchet toward the door.

"Wait! Just give me a chance!" Ratchet pleaded.

"Sorry," Qwark said, but he was obviously not at all sorry. "No time. Galaxy in jeopardy! Get back out there, and remember—you can do anything . . . as long as you're me." With an arrogant grin, Qwark yelled, "*Next!*"

CHAPTER FOUR

BACK AT DREK INDUSTRIES, the chairman's evil plans to destroy his next planet were taking shape.

"Dr. Nefarious!" Drek boomed, stepping into Nefarious's lab. Victor and Zed trailed after him. "The mad scientist who made all of this possible!"

Nefarious cackled ominously as he studied a holographic recreation of the Solana Galaxy. He smiled wickedly as he pulled up an image of the Galactic Rangers on his screen. "'Mad' suggests cognitive impairment," Nefarious said, drumming his fingers together. "I'm more of a vengeful scientist. I trust you're here to meet the troops?"

Drek and his assistants eagerly followed Nefarious to the warbot factory floor. The cavernous room was bustling with activity and machinery. Warbots were being assembled and then dropped on conveyor belts to be assigned blasters and uploaded with instructions.

As Drek gazed out at the beautiful sight of his new army, Nefarious said, "Three thousand sentient warbots, built using the finest raritanium in the galaxy and programmed to assassinate the Galactic Rangers."

The foursome watched as finished warbots came off the assembly line at a rate of more than ten per minute.

"Proton-powered," Nefarious explained. "Rust-proof and laser-guided. Each of these perfect creations is an efficient, remorseless killing machine."

Drek's eyes lit up. "'Remorseless killing machine.' Are there any sweeter words?" His wide brow furrowed. "But will they get the job done? I'd hate to have to send you back where I found you." He grinned at Nefarious, the threat hanging in the air between them.

Nefarious seemed unconcerned. He knew his machines would do the trick. He gestured to one of the bots coming off the line.

"State your prime objective," an inspectobot said to the completed warbot.

"Prime objective: destroy Galactic Rangers," the hulking metal warbot droned.

The inspectobot nodded. "Inspection complete. Weapon issued." The warbot was given a Combuster weapon and sent along the line to the holding tank.

"My warbots know every offensive tactic in the Ranger handbook," Nefarious told his boss, urging the others to watch what happened when the warbot reached an image of the Rangers.

"Target acquired," the warbot said, aiming.

Nefarious laughed maniacally. "They won't just *kill* the Rangers—they'll annihilate them!"

Suddenly, a flash of lightning struck the factory. *Fzzzt.* As the bolt struck, the lights clicked off, and all the machinery shut down. The factory went dark.

"Nice," Victor said. "They killed the lights, too."

"Repair bot!" Nefarious screamed.

A small yellow repair bot flew through the factory. Moments later, the lights blazed back on. The line was back up and running in no time. Drek sighed happily.

"Now we're talking," his assistant, Zed, said.

But something strange had happened during the power outage. When the next bot slid into place for its final check, they could see this one was different from the other bots coming off the line. It wasn't huge and hulking. Instead, it was short, round, and much less menacing.

"State prime objective," the inspectobot ordered.

"Hello," the bot said, waving.

The inspectobot scanned the bot's systems. There was something different on the inside of this bot, too. "Defect detected. Preparing for immediate destruction."

"Oh dear!" the little bot said, scuttling off the line. It began scurrying across the factory floor.

"Immediate destruction in three . . . two . . . ," the inspectobot said.

"Ooh!" Drek said when he spotted the escapee. "A defect! Go play, Victor."

Victor smiled, eager for the chance to destroy something. He began crashing through the factory behind the tiny fellow. "I'm coming for you, defect!"

The bot ran as fast as his short legs would carry him,

but Victor was gaining on him. The defective droid dove into a garbage chute. It was his only chance for escape!

As he spilled out on the other side, the little bot toppled and rolled. When he'd righted himself, he quickly assessed his location. His glowing green eyes settled on a line of escape shuttles nearby. He raced for one, hopping into the pilot's seat just as Victor caught up with him.

The small bot pushed a few buttons, and the shuttle blasted away from Drek Industries.

Victor skidded to a stop, pointing his blaster at the departing shuttle. He fired, but the blast glanced harmlessly off the shuttle's wing.

"Argh!" Victor was furious. His mission had been destruction, and he had failed! Victor *hated* to fail.

The defective bot felt the shuttle rock under the force of Victor's blast. "Computer," he ordered. "Set coordinates for the Galactic Ranger home base."

"Destination set for planet Kerwan," the computer replied. "We will never make it, but hey, what are you gonna do?"

The little bot blinked. "Oh dear."

It was too late to turn back now.

CHAPTER FIVE

LATER THAT NIGHT, back on Kyzil Plateau, Ratchet reluctantly returned to the garage after the Ranger tryouts.

"So," Grim said, stepping away from Mr. Micron's ship. "Are you off to save the galaxy?"

Ratchet hung his head, his ears flopping sadly. "Turns out you were right. I should dream smaller."

Grim shook his head. He felt bad for the guy.

Ratchet shot out his swingshot and pulled himself up to the shop's gantry. The giant scaffold that extended from the edge of the building was his favorite place to go when he had things to think about. He could gaze at the stars and the sky and dream of infinite possibilities.

But tonight, thinking about his biggest dreams and

wishes just made him feel awful. Ratchet sighed and lay back on the metal supports. "I'll never be a Ranger . . ."

His moping was interrupted by a loud *boom!* "Wha—?" He gasped, sitting upright. Something bright and blazing was zooming, like an enormous shooting star. It pierced through the clouds and careened into the Kyzil Plateau. An enormous ball of fire erupted from the crash site.

Ratchet leaped up and hopped onboard his rocket sled, racing toward the strange object that had just crash-landed in his backyard. "Whoa," Ratchet muttered, gazing over the wall of the canyon. It was a ship! He activated his swingshot and sailed down into the crater for a closer look.

"Danger detected. Danger detected," the ship's computer droned. "I told you we would not make it, but did you listen to me? No."

Ratchet pulled up close to the ship. "Hello? Anyone in there?"

A plume of smoke shot out of the shuttle's engine. "Whoa!" Ratchet jumped back, ready to clear the scene. But then he spotted something inside the ship—a bot!

The metal bot seemed unconscious. Ratchet knew he had to try to get the little guy out before the whole ship went up in flames. He used his wrench to try to pry the hatch open, but it was stuck. The ship was blazing hot, but Ratchet was determined.

"Prepare for imminent death," the ship's computer announced.

Ratchet shook his head and tugged harder. "There's gotta be a better way to say that," he growled, popping open the ship's hatch. He grabbed the little silver bot out of the pilot's seat, singing, "*Prepare for imminent death*," in a joyous voice. "How's that?" he asked the computer.

The computer replied by beginning its countdown. "Five . . . four . . . three . . ."

Ratchet knew it was time to jet. Holding the bot tightly, he activated his swingshot and flew up and out of the canyon.

Below him, the computer continued, "Two . . . one . . ."

Kaboom!

Flames licked at Ratchet's heels as he sailed upward, cradling the bot safely in his arms.

As soon as they cleared the upper edge of the canyon, Ratchet set the unconscious bot on the ground and inspected it closely. "Hmm . . . no vector shell damage, sister board appears to be intact . . ."

The bot's eyes flew open, glowing green. It sat up quickly, bonking Ratchet on the forehead. "Wah! Ow!"

"I must get to Aleero City," the bot announced, jumping up. It wobbled, swayed, and hit the ground again. "They are in danger!"

"Who is in danger?" Ratchet asked, standing over the bot.

"An army is coming. I must warn them!" the bot said, trying—and failing—to stand once more.

"Hang on," Ratchet said calmly. "Slow down. You've been in a crash." He kneeled beside the little bot. "What do you say we get you back to my garage? I'll run a diagnostic and have you fixed up in no time."

"Thank you," the bot said. "I appreciate the assistance."

"It's no problem," Ratchet assured him with a smile. "So what do I call you?"

"Hmm . . ." The little bot thought for a moment.

"I suppose my proper designation is warbot defect B5429671—"

Ratchet held up a hand, cutting him off. "Maybe I'll just call you Clank. My name is Ratchet." He held out a hand to shake.

But Clank didn't understand. He just stared at Ratchet's hand. "Up and down," Ratchet said, taking Clank's metal hand in his own. He pumped their hands up and down, show-ing the bot how to shake. "Yeah, there you go. You're a natural."

Clank continued to shake. And shake. And shake.

Ratchet laughed and tried to pull his hand away. "Okay, that's enough."

But Clank wasn't getting it. He kept on shaking.

Ratchet grinned at his new pal. "Or just keep shaking. That's cool, too."

When they returned to Grim's garage, Ratchet popped Clank up onto his worktable and started repairing him. After tinkering and tightening for a while, he was pretty sure he had him back in business. "Almost got it, and . . .

there!" He stepped back and looked over his work. "How do you feel?"

"Fully operational," Clank said.

"Sweet," Ratchet said. "So, what are you doing all the way out here in the sticks?"

Clank stood up, this time with no trouble at all. "I am on a mission of galactic importance."

"'Galactic importance'?" Ratchet said, turning to put his tools away. "Oh boy, you must have damaged your CPU. How many fingers am I holding up?" He waggled two fingers in front of Clank's face.

"Two," said Clank. "But I fail to see the relevance of the question. Chairman Drek has built an army of warbots. They are going to assassinate the Galactic Rangers."

Ratchet whistled. "Oh, *that* kind of galactic importance! Why didn't you say so? I can totally help!"

Clank shook his head. "I could not ask a civilian to get involved in something so dangerous."

"I'm not just a civilian," Ratchet protested. "The Rangers are actually my . . . uh, friends! Why do you think I have so many pictures of them?"

Clank gazed around the room at Ratchet's enormous collection of Galactic Ranger posters and trading cards and action figures. "Hmm . . . ," he said. "But why are you not in any of the pictures?"

"Well, someone had to take the photos, right? I mean, come on—I even have a ship!"

Ratchet led Clank down into the garage and waved his arm in front of Mr. Micron's souped-up ship. A piece fell off the wing and clattered to the floor.

Ratchet chuckled sheepishly. "It disassembles so it can infiltrate enemy strongholds." He lifted his brows at Clank. "So . . . whaddya say?"

CHAPTER SIX

BACK AT THE HALL OF HEROES IN ALEERO CITY, Qwark and the other Rangers were feeling less than optimistic about their quest to find a new recruit.

"What are the odds of actually finding a qualified Ranger way out here in the boonies?" Qwark asked the other Rangers as they strolled through the courtyard. "After all, there's nothing the three of us can't handle."

Qwark's leg froze in midair as something latched on to him. "I am your biggest fan!" a kid called Ollie cried. He gazed up at Qwark fondly, hugging his leg as tightly as he could.

"Gah!" Qwark screamed, shaking his leg madly. But Ollie was holding on with all his might. "It's touching me!" Qwark squealed. He couldn't *stand* ordinary folk. "Get it off, get it *off!*"

As Ollie clung to Qwark's leg, the sky above the court-yard went black. A huge ship had soared into the airspace above Aleero City, casting the entire courtyard in shadow.

"An enemy warship!" Qwark gasped. He shook Ollie off his leg, and then kicked him away. "Take cover, citizen!"

Ollie flew through the air, screaming, "I loooooooove you!"

The Rangers all stared up into the sky. Qwark's eyes went wide. The incoming ship was huge. As they watched, its back panel rolled open, and hundreds of Drek's warbots rolled out.

Spreading their arms wide, the enemy troops glided to the ground. As they landed, the warbots drew their Combusters. They spun in circles until they had the Rangers fixed in their line of sight. One by one, the warbots announced, "*Target acquired!*"

Drek's mission to destroy the Galactic Rangers was underway.

Meanwhile, Ratchet and Clank had "borrowed" Mr. Micron's ship and were heading toward Aleero City. The ship still wasn't in perfect condition—pieces kept falling off as they soared through space—but it did the job. Barely.

Ratchet just hoped it would take them as far as Aleero City. They weren't far from the Ranger stronghold now, and he couldn't wait to be the one to warn the Rangers that danger was imminent.

"Hmm . . . ," Clank said, staring at Ratchet.

"What?" Ratchet said, glancing over at the bot.

"Apologies," said Clank. His internal processor was working overtime, running an image of Ratchet through his system. "I have not been able to locate your species in my database."

"I get that a lot," Ratchet said, shrugging. "There aren't many of us left. Not in this galaxy anyway."

Clank blinked, confused.

"I'm a Lombax," Ratchet explained.

"A Lombax? Fascinating."

Ratchet grinned. "Yeah. I crashed on Veldin when I was just a baby. No note, no message, no name . . ." He turned to look at Clank. "Huh. Kinda like you."

The ship's onboard computer beeped. "Approaching destination."

Ratchet's face lit up. "Whoa . . . Aleero City!"

"Yes," Clank agreed. "It certainly is."

Ratchet guided the ship through the clouds and descended into Aleero City. As he drew close to the capital, his face fell. "No way."

The enormous warbot ship was already hovering in the sky above the once-peaceful city. On the ground, a fierce battle was underway. Warbots had overtaken the sky-bridge and were pushing the Galactic Rangers and the Solana troopers back toward the towers. All over the city, citizens were fleeing from the warbots, screaming in terror. It was chaos.

"It is the invasion!" Clank said. "We are too late."

"I totally thought you were making it all up," Ratchet said, gulping. He steered their ship around the city, trying to figure out his next move.

Down on the ground, Qwark was trying to hold his own. A warbot focused on him. "Target acquired," the bot announced.

Qwark stepped toward the warbot, brandishing two blasters. "You knocked on the wrong door, hombre." He blasted the bot and then turned back to two Solana troopers and winked. "How was that? Did that sound cool?"

The troopers both gave him a thumbs-up. But in the next instant, one of the troopers was blasted off his feet and into oblivion.

Qwark cringed. "Oh boy." He refocused his efforts. There was a time for looking cool, and a time for fighting. Right now, it was time to focus on the fight (though Qwark knew it never hurt to look cool while also being a hero . . . that was kind of his thing). He began firing wildly into the crowd of warbots, yelping joyfully every time he hit a target.

Nearby, Brax had a different strategy. *"Hyungh!"* he grunted, shoulder-checking a group of warbots. They all flew up into the air and landed in a heap of crushed metal.

Cora stepped forward to set phase two into action. She soared through the air, slamming into a warbot's chest. Winking, she pressed two plasma grenades onto him, and then jumped out of harm's way. A second later, the entire pile of warbots exploded.

Ka-pow!

Cora landed, giving Brax a high five with her blaster.

"Brax to the max!" Brax grunted.

Overhead, Ratchet could see the action perfectly from inside his borrowed ship. He whooped with each Ranger success. "Awesome!" He couldn't believe he had a front-row seat to watch his heroes defeat the enemy.

But down on the ground, the enemy warship wasn't prepared to concede. Every time one of the warbots was destroyed, another was released from the ship overhead. They had a seemingly endless supply of troops! Still, they were losing too many.

Victor, who had been given the important job of seeing this mission through to success, was becoming furious. Failure was not an option. Drek had put him in charge, and he was going to return home with a victory.

Using his giant metal claw hand, Victor pulled a warbot close. "Bring me the captain's head, or I'll take yours as a replacement." He pushed the warbot away and charged into battle himself. He was ready to destroy the Rangers— no matter what it took.

CHAPTER SEVEN

HIGH ABOVE THE BATTLE, Ratchet was ready to do whatever he could to help the Rangers. This was his chance to prove he had what it took to join them. At the very least, he could prove to Captain Qwark that he wasn't good-for-nothing. His heart counted for something!

Ratchet guided his ship toward the enemy warship, preparing to release a missile. "I got these guys!" He pressed a button, and the missile raced through the air. It corkscrewed, spinning and wavering through the smoky sky.

But suddenly, it veered away from the warship and raced toward the ground. Ratchet watched with horror as the missile went way off track. It hit an enormous golden statue of Captain Qwark and exploded.

The head of the Qwark statue popped off and rolled across the courtyard, coming to a stop right at the real Captain Qwark's feet. In a tinny voice, the head said, "Welcome to the Hall of Her—herroo—"

Qwark stared at the broken statue in horror. This was a *tragedy*!

Up in the sky, Ratchet grimaced. "Whoops," he said, embarrassed. "I must have forgotten to install the targeting software." He brightened, realizing he could repair it with just a couple quick fixes. "Hey!" he called to Clank. "Take the controls for a sec." He dropped to the floor of the ship, digging at the control panel under the dash.

Clank slid into place in front of the control stick. "Oh . . . ," he said. "I . . . um . . ." He had no idea what to do. The ship careened out of control, bouncing against buildings and ships as they raced through the air above the city.

"Ow!" cried Ratchet as he was thrown into the side of the ship. "Hey! What's going on up there?"

Clank craned his neck to try to see out the ship's front window. He was too short, and had no idea how to work the control board. "Well, unfortunately my piloting skills are, shall we say . . . 'slightly underdeveloped.'"

The ship lurched to the side again as they bumped into another building. "Yeah," Ratchet said, righting himself. "I think we can definitely agree on that!" He clutched at two wires, hastily pressing them together before the ship hit anything else. "Okay," he said, climbing back into the pilot's seat. "How's that?"

"Ratchet," Clank said as missiles exploded around their ship, "we are clearly not prepared for this. We should have called the Rangers to warn them of the attack."

Ratchet chuckled. "Ha! Like they'd know who *we* are . . ."

Clank spun his head around to glare at Ratchet. "But you said they were your friends!"

Ratchet's eyes darted from side to side. *Oops.* He had forgotten his little lie from earlier . . . "What?" he said, acting defensive. "I think you're quoting me out of context."

Clank pressed a button on the side of his head. A recording of Ratchet's voice rang out from his internal speaker, loud and clear. *"I'm not just a civilian. The Rangers are actually my . . . uh, friends."*

"Do you record everything I say?" Ratchet asked.

Clank pressed another button. Once again, Ratchet's voice rang out. *"Do you record everything I say?"*

Ratchet rolled his eyes. "Oh, that is so immature."

"Oh, that is so immature," Clank's speaker repeated.

They were so wrapped up in their conversation that they'd forgotten where they were. They looked out the ship's windshield and realized they'd just burst through an enormous billboard for the Galactic Rangers.

"Ahhhh!" Ratchet screamed as the ground rose up to meet them. "We're going down!"

The ship flipped upside down, turned sideways, and gained speed as it raced toward the pavement below. "Your sense of direction . . . ," Clank said as his body was thrown sideways, ". . . is impeccable."

"I can fix this," Ratchet promised. He reached for a lever and yanked it a split second before their ship delivered them to certain death. The thrusters rotated out to stop the ship, and they hovered in midair just above the ground.

Ratchet and Clank were smashed against the inside of the windshield like two bugs. They peeled themselves from the glass and settled back into their seats.

Gazing out the window, Ratchet realized someone had seen their near-miss. It was Ollie, the Rangers' biggest fan. His eyes were wide, and he opened his mouth and screamed, "That was *awesome*!"

Ratchet saluted Ollie, turned the ship upright again, and rocketed back toward the battle. Below them, the Rangers' troops were still fighting hard to keep the warbots at bay. At this point in a battle, the Rangers had usually won easily, so their continued fighting proved just how tough Drek's warbot army was.

"Ratchet, I believe I might have an idea," Clank blurted. "Your weapon package includes a Mag-Booster. I am rewriting the software to isolate the raritanium alloy used to manufacture us."

"Great idea, Clank!" Ratchet said, nodding.

Down in the city, the Galactic Rangers were still struggling—and losing ground every minute. Back to back, they faced the crowds of warbots, trying to keep their attackers from closing in on them. But no matter how hard the Rangers fought, the warbots just kept gaining ground.

"Bring it on," roared Cora, holding her blaster aloft.

"There's too many of them!" Brax said. "Even I can't shoot them all." He grunted and fired into the crowd of warbots. But three against thousands were difficult odds.

"Hold steady, Rangers," Qwark commanded.

The warbots circled closer, like wolves moving in on wounded prey. Victor was right at the front of his troops, eager to bring the battle to an end and a victory to his master. Holding his spinning plasma blades high in the air, he boomed, "Prepare to die, Galactic Losers."

CHAPTER EIGHT

"COME ON, COME ON!" Ratchet urged Clank. If they had any hope of saving his heroes from destruction, they had to get a move on. It was clear to everyone that the Rangers' hopes of victory were disappearing fast.

Clank tapped away at the ship's computer, reprogramming the software to magnetize the ship. He put all the components that made up the warbots into the central processor, and then tapped out a key. Clank pressed a few more buttons and looked up. "Executing command and . . ." He looked to Ratchet. "Engage Mag-Booster."

Ratchet flipped a switch on the dash, and the Mag-Booster roared to life. "Is it working?"

Clank was suddenly pulled out of his seat and drawn to

the ship's ceiling, held there by the power of the enormous magnet on top of the ship. "Whoa! I do believe it is."

With a whoop, Ratchet steered the ship down toward the plaza below. He zoomed low over the crowd of warbots. Ratchet slowed down, swooping over the waves of warbots. One by one, the bots were pulled off their feet. Helpless, the bots were dragged into the air behind Ratchet's ship, unable to fight back against the magnetic pull.

"Huh?" Qwark said, watching as every single one of the warbots was yanked up and into the air by the Mag-Booster on Ratchet's ship.

"Yeah!" Ratchet hollered. The bots stretched out like a long tail behind the ship as Ratchet blasted up and away from the plaza.

"Oh yes," Clank cheered.

Ratchet gunned it. He blasted high up into the sky, traveling so fast the buildings around them seemed to blur together. They had to keep moving or the warbots would make contact with their own ship.

Down below, the people of Aleero City stared up at the

unknown hero who had brought the battle to a sudden close.

"There are three thousand heavily armed warbots gaining on us," Clank said nervously, glancing over at his pilot.

"I know!" Ratchet said, grinning. "Isn't it great?" He pulled Mr. Micron's ship up high above the city, circling and swerving away from the crowd of bots.

Not far ahead, the warship was waiting to bring Drek's troops home. But Ratchet had a different plan in mind. "Get ready to return to sender!" he growled, then blasted straight toward the warship. "Terminate the Mag-Booster on my mark. Three . . . two . . . one . . ." He yanked back on the stick, releasing the ship's magnetic pull. "MARK!"

Just as they were about to crash into the belly of the warship, Ratchet banked and turned their vehicle toward safety. But the warbots kept flying—straight at their own ship! In less than a second, three thousand warbots crashed into the enormous warship. It exploded in a fiery blast, filling the sky with clouds of smoke and debris.

Everyone in Aleero City watched, waiting, to see if the mysterious heroes would emerge from the mission unharmed.

Vroom!

The crowd burst into cheers as Ratchet steered his ship away from the blast and raced back down to the ground. They had made it. He and Clank had saved the day!

The only one who wasn't impressed? "You have got to be kidding me," Victor hissed. Fuming, he sped away from the plaza and leaped into the nearest taxi. He grabbed the taxi driver by the shirt and threw him out of the cab. Then he blasted away before anyone in Aleero City could stop him.

All around the Hall of Heroes, the people of Aleero City cheered wildly as Ratchet and Clank corkscrewed to safety in their borrowed ship.

As soon as Ratchet touched down, he was swarmed. The city's grateful citizens ran to congratulate him and Clank.

As the crowds rushed past Qwark, the captain soaked in their applause. "Ahh . . ." He chuckled, acting modest. He loved nothing more than basking in his fans' adoration after another hard-fought battle. He closed his eyes and held up his hands, relishing the attention.

But no one stopped to congratulate him. Everyone hurried past to see Ratchet and Clank. Qwark opened his eyes, stumped. "Huh?"

Nearby, Ratchet slid open the hatch on his ship. He and Clank spilled out to thunderous applause. Ratchet took it all in. A hero! *He* was a hero!

Qwark watched in irritation. He knew *he* deserved the victory party, not this . . . *nobody*. He'd fought long and hard, he reasoned, and then this peon had swooped in at the last minute and taken credit for the whole battle?

Qwark grimaced. That wasn't how this was supposed to go down! He knew he had to take control of the situation, and fast, or this mess with a civilian was going to get out of hand!

"All right, everyone," Qwark said, stepping in front of the crowd. "Let's give these heroes some breathing room. I'm happy to field all questions on their behalf."

A news reporter stepped forward. "Captain Qwark! I'm Juanita Alvaro. The Blarg have been underground for over fifty years, since their home planet became overpolluted. They've been looking for a new home ever since. Could their return be linked to the destroyed planets?" She held out her microphone, waiting for Qwark's response.

Qwark chuckled. "I think that's being a little alarmist, don't you, Juanita?"

Clank stepped forward and cut in. "Begging your pardon, Captain, but Drek *is* responsible. And his attack today proves that he is only getting started."

The crowd gasped. Captain Qwark rolled his eyes, dismissing Clank entirely. "Now, now, we must all stay calm. Everything is under control!"

"Captain Qwark! Dallas Wannamaker here," another news reporter yelled. "Does this mean you'll be asking these two to join the Rangers?"

Qwark's mouth hung open. "Say what now?" He scanned the faces of the crowd, who were all looking at him with hope and expectation. "Well, I . . . I . . ." He looked over his shoulder to get a closer look at Ratchet and Clank.

Ratchet waved and smiled, and Qwark's fake smile faded only slightly when he realized he *knew* this hero. He had rejected this hero! But he didn't have much choice—the people were expecting it. He turned back to the crowd and gave them a wide smile. "I don't see why not!"

Qwark pulled Ratchet and Clank close as the crowd erupted in applause. Cameras clicked, eager to snap one of the first photos of the new Galactic Rangers. Qwark lifted his two new Rangers high in the air, eager to be a part of the celebration.

Ratchet whooped and hollered, happier than he'd ever been. "Woo-hoo!"

Dallas Wannamaker turned, speaking through his camera to the entire galactic audience. "You heard it here, folks. The search for a new Galactic Ranger is over. Aleero City will never forget the day it was saved by a . . . uh . . . a cat thingy!"

CHAPTER NINE

"HOW DID THIS HAPPEN?" Drek screamed, watching Dallas Wannamaker's live newscast with horror. He flicked off the TV and stared across his desk. "Someone *explain* it to me!"

Both Dr. Nefarious and Victor hung their heads in shame.

"You!" Drek barked at Nefarious. "You're supposed to understand how they think! How did you not see this coming?"

Then he turned his attention to Victor. "And Victor: Do you know how many candidates you beat out for your position? I could have hired the Zeezil Brothers!" Drek raised his fists in the air and shook them for emphasis. "It's enough to make me want to *vaporize* someone! We're putting our project on hold. I'm ordering all remaining warbots to the Deplanetizer until the heat dies down."

Drek dropped his head to his desk. He was disgusted, humiliated, and crushed.

Nefarious shifted uncomfortably. He wasn't prepared to concede. He knew they could still win if they switched tactics slightly. "Before we make any rash decisions," he began, "I wonder if you'd permit me to troubleshoot this for you?"

Drek didn't lift his head off the table. "Go on," he muttered.

"Our question is simple," Nefarious went on. "How do you destroy a team of heroes?"

Sensing his chance to break in with an idea of his own, Victor blurted out, "Ooh, ooh, ooh, ooh! Well, lots of ways, really. Chains and knives are good. Poison, bombs, an enormous rock . . ." When no one said anything, Victor repeated, "Rock."

Drek lifted his head and glared at Victor.

"The answer is: from within," Nefarious went on. He swooped his arms into the air, looking every bit the mad scientist as he stormed around Drek's office. "If we continue to fight them with muscle, we'll lose every time. But if we turn one of their own against them . . ."

Nefarious wrapped one spindly arm around Drek and spun him around until he was facing the TV screen. The image of Captain Qwark was frozen, paused, on the screen. "Of course, we'd need a weak link. A sad simpleton who would believe whatever we tell him. Someone easy to corrupt. But who?" Nefarious paused, waiting for Drek to figure out where he was going with his little speech. "Who?"

A frozen image of Captain Qwark continued to scowl down at them from the TV. Drek drummed his fingers on his chin, considering the options.

"Who?" Nefarious said, pointing casually at the TV.

Drek still wasn't getting it.

"*Who?!*" Nefarious snapped his fingers and pointed very obviously at Qwark on the TV screen.

"Hmmm," Drek said, his eyes suddenly focusing on the image of Captain Qwark. "I'm getting an idea, boys!" He, too, pointed at Qwark on the screen and laughed maniacally.

"You're a genius, sir," said Dr. Nefarious.

Back in Aleero City, Brax led Ratchet and Clank through the lobby of the Hall of Heroes. "Our training program usually lasts a full year, but we've been cleared to attack Drek Industries in three days," he explained to them. "That means you two are getting the accelerated course."

Ratchet leaned in to whisper to Clank. "We're going to be trained by Brax Lectrus?! This guy's a legend!"

Clank looked up at Brax. "I do not suppose you offer introductory courses in aviation?"

Brax waved his enormous Combuster gun in the air, pointing it casually at Clank like it was an extension of his arm. "No offense, little guy, but I don't think flying's really your thing. Captain Qwark suggested we put you in a position a little less . . ." He trailed off.

Clank peered around the edge of Brax's blaster. "Dangerous?" he inquired.

Brax grinned and nodded.

The three continued through the Hall of Heroes to the team's intelligence center. The intelligence center was stuffed full of brooms and mops. It was very obviously a repurposed broom closet.

Inside the intelligence center, a teenage girl named Elaris was standing up, playing video games at her station.

"Ha!" she taunted, adjusting her headset. "That's right, Lives-at-home-472. What's the matter? Don't like getting beaten? What, are you gonna cry to your mommy?" She stopped short as the sound of wailing came through her earpiece. "Wait, are you really crying?"

"Hey, Elaris," Brax said, knocking on the inside of the door.

"Hi, Brax!" Elaris spun around with a friendly smile. She nodded at Clank. "Is that my new assistant?"

"Greetings," Clank replied. "Your office is . . . most impressive?"

Elaris looked around her "office" and grimaced.

Brax turned to Ratchet and Clank. "Elaris is in charge of developing our gear and providing technical support."

"Usually it's the former," Elaris explained. "The Rangers are the shoot-first-think-later type." She stopped, realizing that probably sounded like they didn't think before acting . . . which they didn't, but the Rangers all refused to admit it. "I'm sorry, Brax. I didn't mean it to sound like that."

Brax played with his gun, distracted. "Like what, now?"

Elaris smirked. "Come on. I'll show you around," she told Clank.

Drek—the leader of the aliens known as the Blarg—had a plan. He wanted to use his mega-weapon, the Deplanetizer, to destroy planets in the Solana Galaxy.

Elsewhere in the galaxy, a Lombax named Ratchet had a different plan. He dreamed of joining the Galactic Rangers, a group of heroes dedicated to protecting the citizens of Veldin and other planets.

But the Rangers' leader, Captain Qwark, told Ratchet he didn't have what it took to become a Galactic Ranger.

All that changed when Ratchet rescued Clank, a tiny robot who'd escaped from Drek's factory.

The two new friends rushed to warn the Rangers that Drek was planning to attack Aleero City. Together, they rescued the Rangers and saved the city.

Now Qwark had to ask Ratchet and Clank to join the Rangers. Ratchet couldn't believe his good luck.

But Drek and his henchman, Dr. Nefarious, had a devious new plan. They wanted to trick Captain Qwark into betraying the other Rangers!

Their plan worked. Qwark sabotaged the Rangers, and Drek captured Ratchet!

Can Ratchet and Clank bring Qwark back to the Rangers—and stop Drek and Dr. Nefarious for good?

Brax led Ratchet back out the door. "Let's go, cadet. Time to make you a Ranger."

Ratchet followed Brax eagerly out into the hall. Then he realized he'd left his pal without saying good-bye. He leaned back into Elaris's office and called out, "I'll see you in a bit!"

Farther down the hall, a door slid open to reveal the Rangers' training room. Brax thumped Ratchet on the back and pushed him inside. "Well, good luck!" he yelled as the doors slid shut again.

Ratchet gazed around the room, letting his eyes adjust to the darkness. A teleporter lowered to the floor, and Ratchet stepped on to it. He was lifted into the air and brought up to the level of the other Rangers, who were all sitting behind a glass panel, watching him.

"Welcome, cadet!" Qwark said. "Let's get you into your new protosuit."

A flashy blue-and-orange suit automatically fitted itself to Ratchet's body, leaving him encased in full-body armor that would help keep him safe during battle. "Your proto-suit is the most advanced combat armor on the market," Qwark told him. "And it comes in the latest fall colors!"

"Sweet . . . ," Ratchet said, looking himself over. He'd never looked quite so *sleek* in all his life. This sure beat his usual uniform back at the garage!

"A neural sensor in your helmet reads your thoughts and telequips the desired weapon into your hands," Qwark said.

Ratchet squirmed inside his stellar new armor, trying to get used to the feel of it.

"Try equipping your Combuster," Qwark urged.

Ratchet focused on a Combuster hanging across the room, hoping his new suit would work the way it was supposed to. He concentrated on how badly he needed the Combuster, held out his hand, and waited.

Nothing.

He squinted and refocused.

Nothing.

Finally, after several long seconds, the Combuster flew through the air and landed right in Ratchet's hand. "Wicked!"

Qwark nodded his reluctant approval. "The Combuster is the backbone of the Rangers' arsenal, allowing you to hit targets in a short to medium range."

Ratchet couldn't wait to try it out. He fired the

Combuster across the room—and felt himself fly backward from the kickback. "Whoa! Ahhh!"

Cora groaned. "This is embarrassing."

"Let's move on to the Alpha Disruptor," Qwark said, pointing to an enormous green-and-silver gun. "It fires a deadly stream of plasma, allowing you to hit multiple targets at once."

Ratchet tried it out, discovering he would need a lot more practice before he could use the Alpha Disruptor in battle. He bounced and careened around the room as a wild stream of plasma rocketed out of his weapon. "Whoa! Wh-wh-whoa!"

"See?" Qwark cringed. "He's got it . . . sort of." He decided it was best to move on to the next tool. "Okay, this little baby is the Negotiator. Fires multiple long-range, high-impact rockets. Great versus heavy armor."

Ratchet gripped the yellow-and-black gun. He braced himself, and then fired. Again, he was knocked off his feet by the force of the gun. "Whaaaa!"

Qwark covered his eyes. Then he introduced the next weapon in the Rangers' arsenal. "Buzz Blades!"

The Buzz Blades nearly buzzed Ratchet's head right off.

"The Warmonger!" Qwark announced.

Ratchet successfully fired multiple rockets out of the Warmonger, feeling satisfied that he'd finally nailed one of his weapons . . . until the rockets turned in midair and chased after him. Ratchet ran for cover.

"The Spiral of Death!" Qwark called out, sighing. He had a feeling he knew where this was headed.

Ratchet blasted a blade out of the weapon . . . and then ducked as it, too, spun off in the wrong direction. "Whoa!"

"Fusion Grenade?" Qwark muttered.

Ratchet tossed the grenade into the air, and it bounced back into his hand. "Look out!" he yelped, flinging himself against the office's glass window.

The three Rangers shared a look.

"Dude," Brax said, summing up the situation perfectly.

"How am I doing?" Ratchet squeaked. He smiled sheepishly as his body slid down the glass.

The looks on the other Rangers' faces said it all: Ratchet was *not* cut out for this.

CHAPTER TEN

"IS THIS REALLY YOUR OFFICE, ELARIS?" Clank asked, scrutinizing the contents of the broom closet carefully. It was packed full of cleaning tools, miscellaneous junk, and a whole bunch of equipment.

Elaris shrugged. "Budget cutbacks. I don't mind it as much as the last guy who had this job—Dr. Nefarious." She pointed at a poster of Nefarious, who was looking every bit as creepy and evil as always. "This place drove him crazy. Literally. He turned evil. The Rangers had to put him in jail. He died in a prison breakout." Elaris stopped and grinned madly at Clank. Then she blinked. "Don't worry. That won't happen to me."

Elaris turned back to her computer, where she had been studying holograms of the recently destroyed planets. "Hmm . . . ," Elaris said, zooming in on one. She clicked over to another, and another. The pieces of the destroyed planets had been gathered from around the gallery and then fitted back together like a jigsaw puzzle. But there was a giant piece of each of the destroyed planets missing.

"What is it?" Clank asked, coming in closer.

"I'm running a simulation based on the fragments we located from each destroyed planet," Elaris explained. "Each one of the planets is missing a famous landmass."

"Well," Clank said, "perhaps the pieces are still out there. There is a lot of space in space."

Elaris chuckled. "I guess. But it's worth bringing up to the captain, don't you think?"

A ruckus in the hall put Elaris on guard. She and Clank spun around just as the office door flew open.

Qwark and Ratchet zoomed into the room, propelled along the ceiling by jet packs.

"Just relax!" Qwark said, swooping up and around, leaving a colorful trail of smoke in his wake. "Everyone stay calm! Something epic is happening!"

Ratchet blasted upward and beamed down at Clank. "Pretty cool, huh, Clank?"

"That's the stuff," Qwark said, puffing his chest out. "Flying in the air like a majestic bird! A majestic bird who knows every fighting style. Watch the master!" He zipped out the office door and executed a few cool flips in midair. Ratchet laughed, delighted.

"Captain," Clank said, trying to get Qwark's attention. "Elaris and I have some information—"

"Can't talk," Qwark said, blasting up into the air again. The air outside the office was filled with smoke from the jet pack. "Doing a fly-by!"

"Sir, if you could come down and speak to us for three minutes . . . ," Elaris pleaded.

Qwark zoomed into Elaris's office as the sprinklers out in the hall turned on. "*Annnnnd* there are the sprinklers," he said, grinning. "But hey, good news!" He pointed finger guns at Elaris. "You already have a mop! So there's that."

"Please," Clank tried again. "If we could just have a minute to discuss our findings—"

Qwark shushed him. "The only thing I'm interested in finding is the Hall of Heroes cafeteria." He nudged Ratchet out of the room. "Let's go, cadet. It's three floors up, and it's meat-loaf day!" He blasted up toward the ceiling at full speed. "Meat loaf!"

Qwark plowed straight through the ceiling. Ratchet eagerly followed him.

Elaris and Clank stared after them. So much for sharing their strange new findings with the captain. Information couldn't compete with meat loaf.

Elaris's shoulders slumped—and then slumped farther when the lights in her office flickered and went out.

"Do they always treat you so poorly?" Clank asked her.

"No," Elaris said. Then, more quietly, she said, "Uh, yes . . ."

That afternoon, Ratchet and Clank stepped outside for a break from their first day of training. As soon as Ratchet hit the street, his fans swooped in to cheer and wave to him.

"Ratchet!" someone called from a car. "We love you!"

Ratchet waved at everyone driving by. They all cheered and honked and cried his name. "Boy," he said, grinning. "For a big city, the people here sure are friendly."

"And loud." Clank scowled.

Ratchet wasn't going to let his little buddy's complaints

bring him down. It felt amazing to be recognized and loved. This whole day was a dream come true.

An aluminum can flew out of the window of a passing car and bonked Clank on the head. "Hey!" yelped Clank.

"Sorry!" the driver of the car called out. "I thought you were a trash can."

"Indeed," Clank said, rubbing his head.

They turned a corner, and Ratchet froze in his tracks. For there, hanging high above Aleero City, was an enormous jumbotron featuring the Galactic Rangers—and he was in the picture! Wearing his protosuit, striking a pose, and looking like he *belonged*! Him . . . Ratchet! One of the Galactic Rangers!

"Wow," he marveled. "Look at that. What do you know, Clank? I'm famous."

"Yes," Clank agreed. "Though I am sure it is exciting, my cultural database shows that fame is highly overrated and ultimately not rewarding. Would you agree?"

"Oh, totally," Ratchet said, distracted. "Way overrated." He turned to Clank, his eyes brimming with hope. "Hey, do you think they'll name a street after me? Or a cologne? *Ratchet: Smell like a hero!*"

As Clank considered this, a group of fans spotted them. The adoring crowd rushed toward Ratchet, reaching out to touch him and get his autograph.

"Easy now," Ratchet said, smiling at everyone. "There's no rush." He took someone's autograph book and began to sign it. "Believe me, I could do this all day!"

But before Ratchet could finish signing his name, Qwark's huge hand grabbed the book from Ratchet and tossed it into traffic. It hit a car, sending pages of autographs flying everywhere.

"Sorry, folks," Qwark said, stepping forward. "But unfortunately, we don't have time for this nonsense. I'm about to reveal my awesome plan for the attack on Drek Industries." He paused momentarily, surveying the crowd. "Unless anyone would like *my* autograph?"

The crowd responded with blank stares and silence.

Qwark laughed uneasily. "Well, that's good. Because we don't have time." He grabbed Ratchet by the collar and dragged him past the crowd of fans. It was time to finalize the Rangers' counterattack!

CHAPTER ELEVEN

INSIDE THE WAR ROOM, Cora, Brax, Elaris, and Ratchet listened to Qwark's plan for attacking Drek Industries. Their captain illustrated his words with silly pictures he had drawn in crayon.

"First, we HALO drop into Skorg City . . . fire a whole mess o' bullets . . . and take Drek into custody so we can be home in time for waffles!" He beamed at the other Rangers as a picture of waffles flashed up on the screen.

Everyone cheered—except for Clank and Elaris.

"Wait . . . ," Elaris said skeptically. "*That* is our plan?"

Qwark puffed out his chest. "Yes, it is."

"Pardon me, Captain," Clank said. "But Chairman Drek is cunning. He will be prepared for our assault."

Qwark groaned. "Look, I think it is beyond adorable that you decided to do all this homework. But big heroes do big things." He winked at Ratchet. "Each second we waste talking is a second Drek could use to destroy another planet."

"But wouldn't it be worth taking five minutes to review our plan?" Elaris argued. "We have holo-schematics, a full workup on the warbots—"

Brax cut her off. "Does anyone else feel like we should have shot something by now? Because it feels like we should have shot something by now!"

Cora raised her hands. "Thank you!"

"Let's take a vote," Qwark said diplomatically. "All those in favor of kicking in Drek's door with a massive arsenal and restoring peace to a galaxy in turmoil, say 'aye.' "

Brax, Cora, and Ratchet all hollered, "Aye!"

Qwark smiled at Clank and Elaris. "And all those in favor of nerding it up here with some pie charts, say 'nay.' "

"Nay," Clank and Elaris muttered.

"Motion passes," Qwark said, pounding the table with his fist. "We assault Drek Industries tonight!"

*　　*　　*

That night, the Rangers were hurtling through the galaxy on the *Starship Phoenix*. They'd reached their final approach to Drek Industries. It was go time.

"Lock and load, Rangers!" Qwark commanded. "Suit up and rally in the aft airlock."

Ratchet prepared for his first battle as a Ranger. His visor was engaged. Clank was strapped to his back. The little bot had been retrofitted as a jet pack so he, too, could be useful on the mission.

"Although I am happy to help with the mission in any capacity," Clank said, "I find this arrangement slightly . . . embarrassing."

Elaris shrugged, tightening his straps. "Sorry, but you're the only one who's been inside Drek's warbot factory."

"Besides, this is the best way for you to keep up," Ratchet added. He wiggled his back, jostling Clank around playfully.

"Remember, your thrusters are powered by Ratchet's suit," Elaris told Clank. "So don't try any solo flights, okay?"

Clank nodded. "I shall endeavor to remember—"

Ratchet grinned at Elaris. "He's in good hands, Elaris."

Qwark strolled into the airlock and shot Clank an irritated look. "You sure you want to take the, uh, extra baggage, cadet?" He smiled apologetically. "No offense, but we're dropping straight into a cauldron. And do you know what's inside that cauldron?"

Brax marched past them. "Is it danger?" he guessed.

Qwark leaned in close. "It's . . . yes, it's danger."

Qwark stepped on to the airlock switch. As soon as he released the button, the Rangers would be dropped out of their ship and left hanging midair. Then it would be up to each one of them to find their own way into Drek Industries safely.

"All right, team!" Qwark called, clapping his hands for attention. "Let's bring it in. Remember, our target is Chairman Drek. Ready, Rangers? On the count of three . . ."

Ratchet felt the floor drop out from under him. He looked up and saw the belly of their ship, hanging open. He was falling!

Qwark chuckled. "Three!"

The Rangers' jet packs roared to life. Ratchet fired up Clank. "All right, pal. Ready?"

"Well . . . ," Clank said. But it was too late to turn around now. They were on their way!

The Rangers all landed in different parts of the Drek office building, as planned. Qwark slid down the edge of a hallway, speaking with the rest of the team through his communicator. "I'm in. Any sign of Drek?"

From the factory floor, Brax said, "Negative. Place looks deserted."

In another hallway, Ratchet, Clank, and Cora were also alone. It was bizarre—there was no sign of life anywhere.

"My internal coordinate system indicates a right turn up ahead," Clank told Cora and Ratchet.

"Eh," Ratchet said. "My gut says *this* way, Clank." He pointed left.

"Glad you're getting in touch with your feelings, newbie," said Cora. "But we're turning right."

"Because . . . ?" Ratchet asked.

Cora scowled at him. "Because I'm your senior Ranger and I say so, that's why."

"Okay! Okay . . . ," Ratchet said, rolling his eyes. Under his breath, he muttered, "Sheesh, cranky."

"What's that?" Cora snapped.

"Huh?" Ratchet said innocently. "I said, er, 'thank ye'—for those words of wisdom!"

"Good save," Clank whispered. He kept his eyes focused as they made their way down empty corridor after empty corridor. "This feels too easy," he said after a while. "Why was there no alarm?"

"It is strange," Cora agreed. "Everyone, stay sharp."

Little did the Rangers know, they *had* been spotted. Drek was watching their every move on his office monitors. He turned to Zed. "Initiate Phase One! Let's scatter the cockroaches. Mwah-ha-ha!" he cackled.

"Mwah-ha!" Zed cackled, mimicking his boss.

Drek cackled louder still. "Mwah-ha-ha-ha!"

"Mwah-ha-ha-HA!" Zed said triumphantly.

Drek slammed his fist to his desk. *"Just push the button, Zed!"*

Soon the Rangers would be eliminated. And then there would be nothing standing in Drek's way!

CHAPTER TWELVE

"ANYONE HEAR THAT?" Qwark whispered into his communicator.

A faint sound rose and fell around him. Qwark spun around, on alert. Something buzzed past him, but he saw nothing.

Cora, Ratchet, and Clank were experiencing the same thing. A tiny something whooshed past Ratchet's ear, buzzing and humming like a swarm of mechanical bees.

"Engaging motion scan," Cora said. She turned on the motion sensor in her visor. Little pricks of red light indicated that she and Ratchet were surrounded . . . by something. But whatever it was was very good at hiding in the shadows. "I'm getting something . . . ," she told the others.

"Yeah," Brax said. "Me, too."

"Zurkon, zurkon, zurkon, zurkon, zurkon . . . ," a tiny

chorus of voices sang. Ratchet jumped as dozens of tiny, flying robots swarmed them.

"Yoo-hoo!" the things called in unison. "Mr. Zurkon is looking to kill you!"

"Zurkons!" Cora screamed. She ducked and weaved, trying to escape the floating robot army. She and Ratchet ran around a corner, firing their lasers back at the Zurkons.

Through their communicators, they could hear Brax dealing with his attacking fleet of Zurkons in his own way. "Ha!" he cheered, igniting his jet pack and flying straight into the swarm. He blasted them, sending dozens of the creepy robots sailing through the air. "Boom, baby! You like that?" He nailed them with a continuous blaster stream. "Who wants a second helping? All you can eat—ha!"

"What's a Zurkon?" Ratchet asked, firing his laser as he and Cora raced toward a door at the end of the hall.

"Robotic bodyguards!" Cora shouted back. "They pro-tect whoever deploys them."

"Mr. Zurkon hates Galactic Rangers!" the Zurkons droned.

Ratchet and Cora raced through the doorway. The Zurkons were right behind them. Ratchet spun around, yelling at Cora, "Watch out!" He aimed his laser over her head, pointing it straight at the door's CLOSE button. He fired.

"Nice shot," Cora said as the door slammed shut. "But if you do that again, I'll shoot you myself."

She looked around their new hiding spot. It was a control room filled with monitors and keyboards. "What is this place?"

"If I may . . . ," Clank began. He stepped forward and began pushing buttons. *This* was the kind of mission Clank could get excited about!

Not far away, Qwark was still swatting helplessly at the fleet of Zurkons attacking him. "Gah!" he shrieked, fleeing the tiny robots as fast as he could.

"Yoo-hoo!" the Zurkons called out.

Qwark began firing his laser at the little pests. The Zurkons pressed forward, and Qwark stepped back.

Suddenly, a set of sliding doors whooshed shut, separating Qwark from his attackers. Chairman Drek was there, standing before a wall of screens.

Qwark grinned. Here it was: his moment. "Don't. Move," he warned, pointing his blaster straight at Drek's head.

Ping! One of Victor's plasma blades zipped through the office and sliced Qwark's gun in half.

Qwark stared openmouthed at what remained of his weapon. He gulped when Victor lurched toward him from the shadows. He knew he was at a disadvantage here. Quietly, Qwark said, "I'm listening."

Drek wheeled around to face his nemesis. "Captain Qwark," he drawled. "I've been watching you these past few days. And I think it's simply dreadful what Ratchet has done to you. He's made people forget who the *real* hero is." He pressed a button on his tablet, activating all the monitors on the walls. Every single one was filled with images of Ratchet being interviewed by reporters, swarmed by fans, taking all the attention usually reserved for Qwark.

Drek smiled sweetly. "Poor old Copernicus Qwark. All you wanted to do was protect the galaxy. And how do they repay you? By dropping you for some . . . well, I don't even know *what* that creature is."

Qwark shook his head. "Even if that were true, I could never betray the citizens of Solana."

"My friend!" Drek boomed. "Betraying them is how you get them to *love* you!" He clapped, and a team of Blarg dressed in suits and ties streamed into the room. "Allow me to introduce you to my team of Blargian public relations professionals. Lads, tell him how we work our magic!"

One by one, the PR pros shouted ideas at Captain Qwark. Ideas for how to make him more beloved, more popular, more *famous*.

"*You're* the victim here!" shouted the first.

"That Lombax *pushed* you to do this!" the second added.

"He did?" Qwark marveled.

"You were desperate, emotionally scarred, depressed even!" the first went on.

"You didn't know what you were doing," agreed the second. "The betrayal was a cry for help."

"It was?" whispered Qwark, becoming convinced.

"It *will* be!" insisted a third PR pro. "A tell-all book, a few guest appearances . . ."

The first widened his eyes. "A holo-film!" An image of a Captain Qwark movie poster filled the wall screens.

"No!" the PR pro barked. "A trilogy!"

"In six months' time, you won't just be Captain Qwark the hero . . . ," the second droned.

"You'll be Captain Qwark, the *survivor*!" finished the third.

"No one needs to get hurt, Captain," said Drek. "We can evacuate the planet and give these people a new place to live. A better place to live." He held a contract in front of Qwark. "So what do you say? Do we have a deal?"

Elsewhere in Drek Industries, Clank was working furiously to crack into the computer system while Ratchet and Cora guarded the doors of their hideout.

Suddenly, the monitors in the room roared to life. Images of an enormous machine filled the screens.

"Hmm," Clank said. "Fascinating. These are plans for something called a 'Deplanetizer.'"

"Deplanetizer?" Cora asked, coming closer.

"Why would Drek be destroying planets?" Ratchet asked.

"Not destroy," Clank said, pushing more buttons. "It seems that Drek is trying to *build* the perfect planet."

CHAPTER THIRTEEN

"HEY! WAIT FOR ME!" Drek's humble assistant, Zed, chased after his boss.

Now that Drek had convinced Captain Qwark to come and work for him, Drek and Victor needed to make a quick escape before the other Rangers got to them. It was time to put Phase Two of their plan into action. Qwark was back with the Rangers, armed with a *new* set of instructions.

Victor blasted off in his escape pod. Drek pushed frantically at his launch button, trying to blast off before Zed could hop onboard. The little guy was baggage, and Drek didn't need a liability.

"Wait! Waaaaait!" Zed squealed.

"Sorry, Zed," Drek said, smiling through the pod's window. "I'll write you an excellent letter of recommendation."

"You don't even have my email," Zed pleaded.

Drek fired up the pod and took off, leaving Zed behind.

Crestfallen, Drek's assistant turned and began to skulk away to figure out a plan. But before he made it more than a few steps, the Rangers had him surrounded at gunpoint.

"Hi," Zed said, waving feebly. "Before you start in with the, uh, questioning, it's important that you understand that I am faithful to my employer."

Cora grabbed Zed and dragged him up to the roof. She dangled him high above the ground, threatening his life if he failed to do as they asked.

Zed began talking. Fast. But ten minutes later, he still hadn't gotten to the point. ". . . and that's how I found out I was lactose intolerant, though I think the parakeet would have died anyway because he was always flying into the window, which is why I got a goldfish . . ."

Brax, Ratchet, Qwark, and Clank watched as Cora continued her interrogation. Ratchet looked at Zed nervously. "She wouldn't drop him, would she?"

"Nah," Brax grunted. "Well . . . maybe."

Zed was still rambling on. Fed up, Cora cut him off. "That's enough! When I said tell us everything, I meant Drek's target list." She shook him, and Zed squealed. "Now, out with it!"

"I would be more than happy to supply you with the target list," Zed offered. "But unfortunately, I signed a legally binding nondisclosure agreement."

"I want the rest of his targets!" Cora growled into Zed's face. "Now!"

"Please," Zed begged. "This was supposed to be a temp job until I got my singing career on track."

Cora loosened her grip on Zed's ankle. He slipped, sliding farther off the edge of the building. "Whaaaa!" he screamed. Breathing heavily, he said, "Okay, okay. It's Novalis. He wants Novalis."

Cora gasped. "Novalis?" She turned to the other Rangers, her eyes wide. "But Novalis is populated."

"Yes!" Zed agreed. "Forty-three million, six hundred and eighteen thousand, nine hundred and twenty-four people to be exact." He blinked and added, "The Schnorkelsons just had twins this morning."

Cora turned to the rest of the Rangers, her eyes blazing. "We've gotta move!"

A short while later, the Rangers were back on the *Starship Phoenix*. They had set their coordinates for Novalis. They had to hustle if they were to have any hope of stopping Drek's next attack.

Deep inside the ship, Zed was singing to himself inside his holding cell.

Casually, Captain Qwark sauntered past his cell, whistling.

"Hey!" Zed yelped when he saw him. "Captain Qwark! Buddy! Remember me? From Drek's office? When you signed that contract and—"

Qwark reached out and silenced him. "Shhhh . . . ," he said, pressing a finger to his lips. His new mission for bigger and better fame would only work if no one *knew* he was working with the bad guy.

Qwark sneaked through the ship, moving more stealthily than ever once he reached the *Phoenix*'s control room. "General Qwark moves into position," he whispered, plugging a bug into a bundle of wires on the control panel. "Cleverly, he deactivates the weapons system . . . yeah, yeah!" He cheered quietly for himself. "And the crowd goes wild! Qwark is the best guy!"

Meanwhile, on the Deplanetizer, Dr. Nefarious was preparing for his biggest evil scheme yet. He stepped toward his computer, pulling up a document. "Dear diary . . . ," he said, speaking as he typed. "I mean, *journal*. Yes." He cleared his throat and then continued. "Dear journal. I've been having the mood swings again. One minute I'm laughing hysterically, the next minute I'm laughing maniacally." He stopped, considering this. "I guess it's because everything is going exactly according to plan. Soon, I'll be long gone and the entire solar system will be nothing but a giant cloud of dust and gas."

"Excuse me, doctor," a Blarg said, stepping inside the room.

Nefarious jumped up, startled. He spun around, looking sheepish.

"Chairman Drek would like to see you," the Blarg said.

"How long have you been standing there?" Nefarious asked.

"I came in during the part about dust and gas."

"Yes, it's my . . . uh, dietary journal," Nefarious said, thinking quickly. "I keep a very strict record of everything I eat and which foods . . . uh, give me . . ."

"Dust and gas?" the Blarg finished for him.

"Exactly," Nefarious said, shrugging.

By the time the *Starship Phoenix* approached planet Novalis, Cora had already notified the ambassador of the coming attack, and the planet's evacuation plan was already well underway. No one wanted Drek to destroy another planet, but the most important thing was keeping all the residents of Novalis safe—no matter what.

"Fighters, ready to rock!" Cora said over her radio as the Rangers soared toward Novalis in individual fighter jets. "So what's the plan, Captain?"

"Huh?" Qwark said. "The plan? Uh, yes. Here's what we're gonna do, Rangers. I'll go in first and try to reason with this Drek character. See if we can talk this out, mano a mano."

"Talk?" Brax barked through the communicator. "I, uh, I don't follow sir."

"Sir," Cora said. "He's blown up five planets already! I think we're done talking."

Elaris broke in. "Captain, if we can just take thirty seconds, I think I have an idea—"

"Sure," Qwark said, annoyed. "Go ahead."

Elaris launched into her idea. "Well, I was looking at the schematics of the Deplanetizer and it occurred to me that there might be a way to—"

Qwark heaved a sigh. "And . . . mute," he blurted, jabbing at the MUTE button on his communicator. He didn't need to hear Elaris's geeky idea. He knew what he was doing. "I'm goin' in!"

CHAPTER FOURTEEN

INSIDE THE DEPLANETIZER, Drek's troops were keeping a close eye on the approaching Rangers. "Hostile ship on approach, sir," one of Drek's Blarg announced. "Should we fire proton cannons?"

"Not yet. I've got a shiny new puppet down there. And I'm about to put on a show." Drek chuckled. He pressed a button, transmitting a hologram of himself into Qwark's fighter. "Ah, Captain Qwark, you performed marvelously. Be honest—are you a professional actor?"

Qwark beamed. "Well, I *did* dabble in my share of theater back in grade school. Every year I'd play the dad—"

Drek laughed, cutting him off. "An enthralling saga I'd love to hear! But first . . . you've disabled the weapons system on the Rangers' fleet, right? Just as a safety precaution, mind you. We wouldn't want an intense situation to escalate out of control."

Qwark rubbed his chin. "Of course we wouldn't want that! But I have your word that my team isn't going to get hurt, right?"

Drek smiled silkily. "My dear Captain! Where's the trust?" He deactivated the hologram monitor and turned to his minions. With an evil laugh, he ordered, "Destroy them all!"

The Rangers soared toward the Deplanetizer. Suddenly, Cora spotted something troubling up ahead. "Contact! Contact!" she yelled into her communicator.

There were dozens of Blarg fighters heading straight toward them. The Rangers were *way* outnumbered. "All units, engage!"

Brax, Cora, and Ratchet aimed their weapons at the attacking ships and squeezed their triggers. Nothing happened.

"Error, error," the computer droned. "Weapon system compromised."

"Cannons! Missiles!" Brax shouted, pressing all his weapon buttons. "Weapon systems are negative across the board!"

"Same here. I got nothing," Cora confirmed.

"We've been sabotaged!" Elaris said.

"Rangers, fall back!" ordered Cora.

"Break off!" Brax said, executing a sharp turn away from the Deplanetizer. The Blarg fighters chased after them, firing a constant stream of missiles. "Break off!"

Drek watched the action on his monitors, growing more excited by the minute. "The Rangers are retreating, sir," one of his aides announced.

"Brilliant," Drek said, grinning.

Victor stepped forward and surveyed the monitors carefully. He looked at the Rangers' *Starship Phoenix*, and then turned to one of Drek's minions. "Get me a holo-scan of that ship."

The aide leaped up to comply. "Right away, sir!" He pulled up an image of the *Phoenix*, including clear pictures of the two Rangers who were still left onboard.

"Enhance," Victor ordered. The Blarg enlarged the image.

Victor glared at the crystal-clear picture of Clank on screen.

Drek gazed at the screen and whistled. "Well, lookie lookie. What have we here?"

"The defect," Victor growled.

"Ah, yes," Drek said. "The one that got away."

"Not this time," Victor said, making his way toward the door.

"Are you sure, Victor? He looks awfully dangerous," Drek taunted.

Victor was furious. He would not fail again. "Teleport me to that ship," he ordered.

A Blarg cowered under Victor's fierce gaze. "It's impossible, sir. It's shielded!"

"Just get me close!" Victor snapped.

The Blarg did as he was told.

Zap! Victor stepped on the teleporter and was gone.

CHAPTER FIFTEEN

"I'VE GOT ENEMY FIGHTERS EVERYWHERE!" Ratchet cried as he and the other Rangers peeled away from Drek's counterattack.

But even as Ratchet spun his ship for an escape, he felt a tug of responsibility. Captain Qwark was on the Deplanetizer, waiting for backup, and Ratchet wasn't about to leave his teammate stranded.

Ratchet shook his head to clear it. "No—no! I can't leave him." He turned on his communicator. "I'm going in!" Ratchet declared. He did a U-turn and headed back toward Drek's ship.

"Ratchet, don't do this," Elaris urged. "If you give us a minute, we can work out an assault plan."

"There's no time!" Ratchet replied. "Captain Qwark is in

there fighting an entire army on his own!" He swerved to avoid oncoming turret fire from the Deplanetizer.

Little did he know, Captain Qwark was doing *just fine* inside the enemy ship. In fact, at that very moment, their noble captain was eating bonbons and getting foot rubs from Drek's Blarg minions. (There were certain benefits that went along with joining the bad-guy team.)

"Their defensive fire is too strong!" Elaris said as Ratchet blasted toward the Deplanetizer at warp speed. "Pull back. Your fighter won't make it!"

"I don't have to land," Ratchet said, hatching a plan inside his head. "I just have to get close . . ." He steered his ship straight into the path of oncoming turret fire. The blasts rocked his ship as he drew closer . . . closer . . .

"Hull integrity at two percent," Ratchet's ship said. "Prepare to teleject."

"Ratchet," Clank said through the communicator. "Please, listen to Elaris. The odds of surviving a head-on assault, given the structural integrity of your ship, is roughly six hundred thousand, nine hundred and ninety-three to one!"

Ratchet gunned his ship again. "Big heroes do big things," he declared.

"Three . . . ," his computer began. "Two . . . one . . ."

Just as his ship was about to explode, Ratchet ejected. His fighter had gotten him just close enough! He sailed through the air, ignited his jet pack, and propelled himself into the Deplanetizer.

"He made it!" Elaris cheered.

Bam! Elaris and Clank both toppled sideways as the *Phoenix* rocked from side to side. A huge blast had hit the ship.

"What was that?" Elaris asked, glancing at Clank.

"I do not know," Clank said. "I will investigate."

He set off toward the back of the ship. Nervously, he glanced toward the door of the airlock. There were muffled banging sounds coming from the other side of the door. Clank crept forward and reached out one hand to investigate. "Probably just the ship settling," he told himself. "Nothing to be alarmed about. Nothing at . . . *ahhhhhhh!*"

The door flew open. Clank's eyes went wide when he saw *Victor* on the other side of the airlock.

With a shriek, Clank tried to slam the door shut again. But Victor was too quick.

"Defect!" Victor screamed, his eyes focusing on Clank. "I am coming for you, defect!"

Victor reached for him, but Clank managed to race away and slam the door of the airlock just in time.

"I believe we may have a problem," Clank said, collapsing on the other side of the door.

Bzzzzz! Suddenly, Victor's Electro-Blade sliced through the airlock door, narrowly missing Clank's head.

Clank jumped up and hurried away.

They definitely had a *big* problem.

Back on the Deplanetizer, Ratchet's communicator buzzed. "Ratchet, where are you?" Elaris's voice crackled through the line.

"Can't talk," Ratchet said quietly. "I'm almost to the control center."

"Captain Qwark did something to our ship," Elaris said. "Nothing's working! And I think Clank's in trouble."

"Roger that," Ratchet said, running through the corridors

as quickly as he could. He raced through the open door into the Deplanetizer's control panel. "As soon as I stop the Deplanetizer from firing at Novalis, I'll be right back to help." He raced toward the giant machine that controlled the Deplanetizer's weaponry.

Overwhelmed, Ratchet studied the panel, trying to figure out which button to push to turn the machine off.

"Deplanetizer is now online," a tinny computer voice called out.

Ratchet scanned the control board again, unaware that Drek was creeping up behind him. As Ratchet focused on the panel, Drek chuckled—then aimed his Mag-Net Gun right at Ratchet's head.

Zzzzzzz! It was a perfect shot. Ratchet flew up into the air, encased in an electric containment sphere. He was trapped!

Drek chuckled, watching with glee as Ratchet struggled to escape. "Bravo, my boy, bravo! I deal with my share of morons on a daily basis, but this? This is seriously next level."

Drek held up a finger, calling two of his security guards forward. "Take him!"

CHAPTER SIXTEEN

MEANWHILE, BACK ON THE *STARSHIP PHOENIX*, Clank had ducked inside a vent to hide from Victor.

"Where are you?!" Victor boomed, searching the *Phoenix*'s corridors. "Come out and fight!"

Clank peeked out from between the slats of the vent just in time to see Elaris launch herself on to Victor's back. "You want a fight? I'll give you a fight!"

Victor hurled her across the room. "No free rides!"

Elaris smashed against a water purifier, cracking it open. Water streamed toward Victor.

Victor eyed the water with alarm.

From inside the vent, Clank monitored Victor's actions with interest. Victor had a weakness: water.

Unfortunately, the moment Clank realized Victor's

weakness, Victor realized where Clank had been hiding. The enormous robot lunged for the vent's cover, tearing it away from the wall—just as Clank fled out the other side! Victor grabbed at him.

Clank dropped to the level below. Victor stormed after him. "Get back here. I'm going to make you wish you were never created!"

Clank dashed across the room, heading for the weapons locker. He tugged at the Thundersmack gun, struggling under the weight of it. Victor sneered as Clank drew near. "You're nothing but a pathetic defect!"

"Perhaps," Clank agreed. "But I am waterproof."

He pulled the trigger. A cloud swelled up to the ceiling of the *Phoenix*, coming to rest over Victor's head. With a clap of thunder, the cloud rained down on him.

"You've outsmarted me for the last time!" Victor said, lunging for Clank.

The moment he moved, electricity crackled across Victor's body. His arm reached out, but when his hand was inches from Clank's body, Victor turned to rust.

"You were right," Clank said. He touched the enormous,

rusted robot with one finger, and Victor's frozen body fell to the floor. "That *was* the last time."

Unfortunately, Ratchet wasn't faring as well as his pal Clank. Drek's minions rolled him along a catwalk inside the Deplanetizer.

"I never had a proper planet," Drek told Ratchet. "I spent my formative years underground, where everything was dark and wet and hot."

As they passed an open door, Ratchet's attention was drawn to the inside of the room. He was startled to see Captain Qwark chatting away with one of Drek's employees!

"Ohhhh," Qwark said awkwardly, seeing Ratchet outside. "Uh, hey there!"

"Qwark?" Ratchet said, confused. Last time he'd heard from the Rangers' captain, Qwark was headed toward the Deplanetizer to stop Drek. But this didn't look like *stopping* him. It looked like Qwark was just hanging out!

"This is . . . uh, awkward." Qwark hastily pushed a button and the door slid closed. Before Ratchet could ask any questions, Drek's minions rolled him away.

"The next time you and those moronic Rangers decide to play hero . . . plan better!" Drek called after him. He turned to his team. "Toss him into one of the shuttles. I want him to live to see his failure!"

"Drek, don't do this," Ratchet pleaded. "Novalis is home to millions!"

"Yes, yes," Drek grumbled. "And they had their time in the sun. Now it's our turn!" He hurried away, shouting, "Commence deplanetization!"

Ratchet tried to fight back. He had to stop Drek! But it was no use. Drek's guards tossed him into an escape shuttle and slammed the door down behind him.

"No!" Ratchet screamed as the shuttle flew out of the Deplanetizer and sailed into open space.

Ratchet watched helplessly as a beam of light shot out of the Deplanetizer, heading straight for Novalis. Ratchet shielded his eyes, the light nearly blinding him.

For a second, it seemed as if everything was going to be fine . . . but then Novalis cracked into hundreds of pieces and exploded. It was too late to save the planet now. Drek had destroyed the beautiful planet, and with it, millions of homes.

The other Rangers watched from their own ships, with matching horrified expressions on each of their faces.

Inside the Deplanetizer, Qwark stared at Novalis as it crumbled into bits. For once, he didn't feel proud of his accomplishment—he felt guilty. What had he helped Drek achieve? What had *he* done?

One of Drek's minions approached and handed him his new Drek Industries ID card.

"Well, here's your ID. Welcome aboard!"

When Qwark didn't respond, the Blarg said, "Captain?"

"Huh?" Qwark said, finally noticing he wasn't alone. "Oh. Yeah. Thanks." His attention was drawn to the door. Someone was walking by his office, humming.

Qwark craned his neck, and then gasped.

It was someone Qwark thought had died long ago—Dr. Nefarious.

Drek watched the destruction of Novalis with tears of joy in his eyes. "Release the harvesters!" he ordered.

Tiny harvester bots flew out of the Deplanetizer and rocketed through space. They floated through the debris surrounding Drek's ship. One by one, they landed on a specific chunk of the former planet. Hundreds of red dots overtook the piece, connecting with one another to cover it completely.

The harvested piece of Novalis began to glow. Then, suddenly, it disappeared.

"Bring in New Quartu!" Drek commanded his Blarg minions a short while later.

Drek watched eagerly as his minions guided Drek's brand-new planet toward their master using the Deplanetizer's laser beams. New Quartu had been carefully constructed using the best parts of each of the destroyed planets. The result? An almost-perfect planet. Drek had just one more piece to harvest, and then he would finally have his dream home.

"It's beautiful," Drek said, weeping with joy.

The Blarg minions watched while Drek had his moment.

"I did it, Father!" Drek said, still weeping. "I did it . . . and it's beautiful!"

CHAPTER SEVENTEEN

"IN THE WAKE OF NOVALIS'S DESTRUCTION and Captain Qwark's shocking betrayal . . . ," Dallas Wannamaker's newscaster voice rang out from the television in Ratchet's loft. Ratchet was there, busily taking down all of his Ranger posters. He had had it with the Galactic Rangers.

Ratchet hadn't been home for long, but it felt like years ago that he had been a part of the Rangers—since he had been the Ranger who had failed to save the day. Ratchet's shoulders fell as he listened to the rest of the news report.

"The president has ordered a galaxy-wide alert to all Solana residents: Residents are to remain in their homes while authorities manage the crisis. And though Novalis was successfully evacuated, the question remains . . . did we put our trust in the wrong Lombax?"

Ratchet flicked the TV off and slumped down on his bed.

"Can I come in?" Using a piece of shop machinery, Grim raised himself up to Ratchet's room.

Ratchet shrugged. Grim stood there quietly, trying to figure out what he could say to make his friend feel better. "That protosuit of yours keeps beeping," he finally said. "All day, all night, voices asking you to come back. Those Ranger hotshots are persistent."

"Thanks, Grim. I'll turn it off in the morning."

Grim took a deep breath, looking around Ratchet's room. The only picture still hanging on the wall was of Grim and Ratchet from many years before, when Ratchet was a young Lombax.

"Hey . . . ," Grim said, pointing at the photo. "I remember this. You wandered into my garage and took my rocket sled for a test drive. No fear, no safety check—you just flipped the switch and off you went. Took three police bots to chase you down and teach you how to stop!" He laughed.

Ratchet did not. He looked over at Grim. "I guess I just wanted to do something *big*. I wanted to *matter*, you know?"

Grim sighed. "Look, I, uh . . . I ain't ever been very good with advice. But I do know this—to be a hero, you don't have to do big things. Just the right ones."

Ratchet brightened slightly. "That's actually not bad."

"Thank you," Grim said with a smile. "I have my moments."

"I thought I might find you here." A voice rang out in the garage, startling Ratchet.

Ratchet stopped sweeping and spun around. "Clank?" he said, surprised to see his friend again. He thought Clank—like the rest of his Ranger life—was long gone. "I'm not going back, Clank. This is where I belong. You were right. Fame is overrated. Especially when you're famous for causing a complete disaster."

"It was not a complete disaster," Clank said.

From inside Grim's office, a voice on the radio blared out, "*Authorities are calling it a 'complete and utter disaster' as cleanup crews endeavor to sift through the—*"

Grim scrambled to turn down the volume. He looked at Ratchet apologetically. "Sorry!"

"The evacuation of Novalis was successful. No one was killed or injured," Clank continued.

"But those people lost their homes," Ratchet protested. "And for that I have to take full responsibility."

"Blaming yourself and taking responsibility are two very different things. If you truly want to be accountable, you will endeavor to make things right the next time," Clank told him.

"Next time?" Ratchet asked.

Clank nodded. "Drek has one more target on his list. With Captain Qwark now working for the enemy, the Rangers need you more than ever." He paused, and then held out one hand to shake. "And I would like to offer my assistance in any way possible . . . partner."

Ratchet reached forward to shake, but instead he was tossed to the ground as something rocked the garage.

"Earthquake!" Grim yelled, taking cover.

"What is that?!" Ratchet said, spinning around.

Clank smiled. "I brought some friends."

A shadow fell over the garage as the *Phoenix* rose up and over the building. Ratchet ran outside just in time to see Elaris, Brax, and Cora step off the Rangers' starship.

"Okay," Cora said, grinning at Ratchet. "Pity party's over. Time to get back to work!"

Ratchet grinned right back at her. Then he turned to face the whole team. "Listen, guys. I'm sorry I ran out on you like that. Even though I messed up, I should've stayed to fix it and see it through."

"Ah," Cora said, shrugging. "We've all made bad choices. Here—check it out." She handed Ratchet her tablet. "My cadet photo."

He glanced at the screen, yelping when he saw a picture of young Cora, with huge over-styled hair and heavy makeup. She looked a million times different from the fierce fighter she was now.

Brax leaned in for a look, and then doubled over with laughter. "Whoa! That is totally tragic. How embarrassing!"

"Oh really?" Cora said, lifting an eyebrow. "That's how we're playing?" She flipped her tablet over to show everyone a picture of a very nerdy, wimpy-looking Brax.

Brax stopped laughing as quickly as he had started. "Okay, everyone chill out! We have a job to do. I need to start shooting at something immediately."

Elaris cut him off. "Well, before we just go off and start shooting at things, I was thinking that . . ." She cut off, noticing that all the Rangers were looking at her as impatiently as they always did when she hatched a plan. "Oh, forget it."

"No, wait," Ratchet said. "Go on. I think we need to hear what you have to say."

Elaris smiled at him. She couldn't believe they were finally going to listen to her! "Well," she said. "It occurred to me that we can't move a *planet* out of the way. But what if we could move the weapon targeting that planet?"

"Move the Deplanetizer?" Ratchet asked.

"Knock it off course," Elaris explained.

"Okay . . . ," Cora said skeptically. "Awesome. And just how are we going to do that?"

Elaris frowned. "I'm not sure yet. But I'm working on it!"

Ratchet glanced around the garage, thinking. His eyes settled on Mr. Micron's ship and the Mag-Booster attached to it.

"Hey," he said, smiling at his friends. "I might have an idea!"

CHAPTER EIGHTEEN

"DREK!" CAPTAIN QWARK BARKED, racing to catch up with his new boss on the bridge of the Deplanetizer. "I want to talk to you. You tried to kill my Rangers! You said you'd leave them alone."

Drek tried to look innocent. "And I meant it at the time! I detest bloodshed as much as any other Blarg, but sometimes sacrifices are necessary for the greater good."

Qwark scowled at him. "I know you're working with Nefarious on this."

"Yes," Drek said happily. "Isn't it wonderful? We're all part of the same dream team. We should make T-shirts!"

"You're making a big mistake," Qwark told him. "You have no idea the kinds of evil Nefarious is capable of!"

Drek shook his head. "Oh, but I do. It's all right here

on his résumé." He pulled out his tablet and flashed Dr. Nefarious's résumé in front of Qwark's face. "Special skills: Horrendous evil. Unspeakable evil. Diabolical evil," he read aloud. "He's very well-rounded." He peeked at the bottom of the résumé, adding, "And apparently, he can juggle!"

Suddenly, a door slid open and Nefarious appeared before them. He tented his fingers together, cocked an eyebrow, and said, "Uh-oh. Do I feel my ears burning?"

Drek clapped. "Ah, there's our little juggling psychopath now."

Qwark stared at Nefarious, his mouth open. He still couldn't believe Nefarious was *here*. On the Deplanetizer. With him! "You . . . but I thought you died in a prison escape! There were witnesses!"

Nefarious smirked. "Oh, people will say and do just about anything for the right price." He brought his face up close to Qwark's. "What was *your* price, Qwark? What was your price for selling out your friends? Your face on another cereal box, perhaps?"

Qwark's face flooded with shame and horror.

Nefarious looked delighted. "Now, why don't you run

along so the chairman and I can get back to the business at hand?"

"But . . . ," Qwark protested. "But what am I supposed to do?"

"You can guard the water cooler . . . with fury!" Drek suggested. He gave Qwark a thumbs-up, and then shoved him out the door.

As soon as Qwark was gone, Drek grinned. "That was fun!" He turned his back to Nefarious, adding, "And T-shirts would be fun, too, don't you think? Good for morale."

Without warning, Nefarious pulled out a weapon and blasted it at Drek . . . who turned into a fluffy, adorable sheep.

Drek the sheep blinked at Nefarious. "*Baa*-zaar."

Nefarious giggled. "The Sheepinator! One of my personal favorites." He waved at Drek the sheep. "It's time for a change of management!"

Nefarious happily dragged sheep-Drek toward a shuttle. He shoved his former boss inside the pod. "You wanted New Quartu, I'll give it to you. Happy trails!" he crooned. He pushed the EJECT button and sent Drek sailing off toward a happy new life on the planet New Quartu.

Nefarious spun around, ready to take the helm of the ship—and the most powerful weapon of all time. "Yes," he whispered. "It's almost here . . . the beginning of the end." He cackled. "Let the games begin!"

Back in Grim's garage, the Rangers were working together to get the *Phoenix* ready for their big mission. Both Grim and Zed—Drek's former assistant—had eagerly chipped in to help with the preparations. Everyone was excited to be a part of the Rangers' team.

"Hey, everybody!" Elaris called out from inside the *Phoenix*. "Get in here. Now!"

The Rangers gathered around Elaris and Clank.

"You're not going to believe this. We finally managed to decode the Deplanetizer plans from Drek Industries. We found out Drek's next target . . . is Umbris," Elaris began.

Cora shrugged. "Well, at least he picked an empty planet this time."

"Yes," Clank said. "However, Umbris is a volatile planet. Its core is made up of pure melluvium. Blowing it up will result in a chain reaction that will destroy the entire galaxy."

"But why would Drek do that?" Ratchet wondered aloud. "I thought he was trying to *build* the perfect planet."

"Well, Umbris was not Drek's idea. Duh," Zed piped up.

"What do you mean?" Cora demanded, spinning around to face off against the small bot.

"It's Nefarious," Zed said.

"*Dr.* Nefarious?" Brax gasped.

"No," Zed teased. "Steve Nefarious." He rolled his robotic eyes. "Of course it's Dr. Nefarious!"

Cora glared at Zed. "Funny how you didn't mention that when I was dangling you over the edge of a building."

"Well, you didn't ask, now, did you?" Zed snapped.

"That's it," Cora said, grabbing a Combuster. "I'm shooting him."

"Wah!" Zed screamed.

"Don't shoot him," Ratchet urged.

"I am confused. I thought Nefarious was dead." Clank looked to Zed for answers.

"Only on the inside," Zed said menacingly. "Otherwise, he's very much . . . *aliiiiive!*"

CHAPTER NINETEEN

LATER THAT DAY, the *Starship Phoenix* hovered in the airspace over Umbris. The Ranger team was armed with a fleet of Solana ships for backup. They were ready to take on Drek and his Deplanetizer once and for all.

Elaris stood before the control board, gazing out the front window of the *Phoenix*. "We are now as close as we can get without being spotted," she told the team.

Ratchet nodded. "Okay, so what's the plan, Elaris?"

"Go on," Brax urged. "We're listening."

"Well," Elaris said. She was happy—and surprised—that someone was finally willing to listen to her ideas. "I've been hard at work on something called the Hologuise." When it was activated, she explained, the Hologuise could make people look exactly like someone else. "For this mission, the Hologuise will project a visual and audible replication of Captain Qwark that is so realistic, it would fool his own mother."

Elaris explained her plan to infiltrate the Deplanetizer to the team. "With Ratchet posing as Qwark, he and Clank will dock on the Deplanetizer. They will easily gain access to the ship by fooling the simple-minded Blarg into thinking Ratchet is Captain Qwark."

She told the Rangers that Ratchet would convince the Blarg guards in the control room to deactivate the shield grid. "Once inside," she explained, "Ratchet and Clank will make their way through the Star Cracker chamber to the inner core. Then, with Clank's internal coordinate system, they will quickly locate the Stabilizer housing unit."

Elaris quickly told them how to open the hatch of the Stabilizer. Ratchet soaked everything in, preparing for the mission ahead. "Once the Stabilizer is exposed, it can easily be disconnected." Elaris took a deep breath, hoping the rest of the team was following along with her plan.

"Hacking into the mainframe computer, Clank will then disable the weapons system, leaving the Deplanetizer completely vulnerable to any outside forces."

She looked around expectantly. It actually seemed like the other Rangers got it! So now it was time for the team to put her plan into action.

First, they activated the Hologuise. Disguised as Captain Qwark, Ratchet—along with Clank, who was strapped to his back—sneaked onboard the Deplanetizer. Just as Elaris had predicted, they easily disconnected the Stabilizer and disabled the weapons system.

In fact, everything went exactly according to Elaris's plan . . . until the very end. That's when things got a bit messy.

Moments after Clank had tapped into the mainframe, the weapons system blasted out a warning. The Blarg minions in the control room of the Deplanetizer freaked out. They ran around the ship, desperate to find Dr. Nefarious.

"Dr. Nefarious!" one of them screamed. "Sir—I mean, doctor!" He paused. "Hey, where are you going?"

Nefarious was climbing into an escape pod.

"Me?" he said, laughing nervously. "Nowhere! Certainly not out of a system-wide blast radius."

"What?" The Blarg gasped.

"What?" Nefarious repeated.

The Blarg shook his head to clear it. "We've been infiltrated," he told Dr. Nefarious. "The Galactic Rangers are trying to shut down the Deplanetizer and I can't find Chairman Drek anywhere!"

Dr. Nefarious stepped away from the escape pod, grumbling to himself. "You want something done right, you have to do it yourself . . ."

While Nefarious worked up a strategy for counterattack against the Rangers, Ratchet continued to proceed full speed ahead with their plan. What he didn't realize was that the Blarg guards had spotted him without his disguise.

Ratchet spoke quietly to the other Rangers through his communicator. "And we're clear! All units, move in!"

"Way to go, you guys!" Elaris cheered.

Clank was the first to realize they were in trouble. "Ratchet!" he warned.

Ratchet spun around.

"Greetings, cadet!" Captain Qwark shouted, using his jet pack to hover ominously over Ratchet and Clank.

"Captain Qwark!" Ratchet hollered. "On behalf of the Galactic Rangers, I'm placing you under arrest."

"You can't do that. I'll just arrest you right back!" Qwark sniped.

"On what charge?" Ratchet demanded.

"False arrest?" Qwark suggested. "Being annoying? Who cares?"

Ratchet narrowed his eyes at Qwark. "You stabbed your own team in the back, Qwark."

Qwark shook his fists at Ratchet and screamed, "Just like you stabbed me in the back. Taking my fans, my sponsors, my lucrative endorsement deals . . . *my parking space!*"

"You were my hero," Ratchet said sadly. "Now you're no better than Nefarious."

Qwark waggled a finger at Ratchet. "How. Dare. You. I am *way* better-looking than Nefarious! Seriously, have you ever seen him up close?"

Ratchet telequipped a small Combuster into his right

hand. "I'm taking you in," he told Qwark. "By force, if necessary."

"Aww . . . ," Qwark cooed. "That's so cute. Wittle Wombax with his wittle gun!"

Ratchet squeezed the trigger. A huge boxing glove sprang out of the end of the Combuster and smashed Qwark in the face.

Qwark rubbed his nose. Then he jumped up, retaliating against Ratchet with a handful of blasters.

As Ratchet tried to avoid Qwark's fire, he shouted, "Qwark, stop! You don't want to do this!"

"Don't tell me what I want to do!" Qwark growled.

Ratchet and Qwark raced around the Star Cracker deck, firing weapons at each other nonstop. "Enough, Qwark. Nefarious is tricking you!" Ratchet yelled, ducking to avoid Qwark's Spiral of Death blaster.

"Oh, that's right," Qwark said. "*You* know everything! Hey, why don't we all listen to Ratchet?"

Ratchet activated his swingshot and pulled himself and Clank out of the way. As they soared upward, Ratchet fired a set of Buzz Blades at Qwark.

The captain easily avoided Ratchet's attack. "Buzz Blades?" Qwark scoffed. "I taught you better than that!"

Ratchet focused, equipping a new weapon. He fired, and gelatinous green creatures oozed toward Qwark. *Splat!* They landed on Qwark's face, rendering him momentarily sightless.

"Gah!" Qwark screeched, swatting at the slime. "Some of it got in my mouth! It's *in my mouth*!"

With Qwark distracted, Ratchet took an opportunity to stop and think. "He's just too good," he told Clank.

Before they could come up with a plan, Ratchet and Clank heard something whirring below. They were both pulled across the platform and tugged through the air. They slid to the edge of the platform.

Below them, a tornado spun wildly, threatening to swallow up Ratchet and Clank if they fell. The force of the tornado pulled them to the edge of the platform, and they tumbled off. Ratchet quickly activated his swingshot, holding tightly to Clank's foot to keep his friend from being sucked into the vortex.

"Tornado Launcher!" Qwark screamed. Then he laughed.

"Nefarious may be a homicidal lunatic, but he sure can build a gun."

"Qwark, please," Ratchet pleaded, clinging to his swing-shot. "You're not a villain. You're not like Nefarious. This isn't you, and you know it!"

The tornado's wind tugged Ratchet's Captain Qwark trading card out of the Lombax's pocket. It fluttered through the air, landing on Qwark's face.

Qwark plucked it off his face and held it out, gazing at a picture of himself from long ago.

"If Umbris is destroyed," Ratchet hollered, "everyone will die, including us! Is that how you want to be remembered?"

Qwark held the trading card, staring at his own face smiling back at him. When this card had been printed, he was a role model, a hero. Now, he was . . . what?

He took a deep breath. He couldn't hurt people like this. He was a Ranger—his job was helping!

Captain Qwark telequipped a blaster into his hand and blew up the Tornado Launcher. The wind stopped, and Ratchet and Clank lowered themselves to the ground.

Captain Qwark approached them, his shoulders slouching. "I'm sorry," he said. "I don't know how things got this far."

Before Ratchet could speak, Dr. Nefarious screamed from overhead, "This is just pathetic!"

Qwark spun around. "Nefarious, give it up. It's over. As head of the Galactic Rangers . . ." He pointed at Ratchet. "*He's* here to place you under arrest."

"Me?!" Ratchet blurted.

"Absolutely," Qwark said. He pointed at Nefarious. "Arrest this man. For his unspeakable crimes against the galaxy."

"My crimes?" Nefarious laughed. "*My* crimes?! The real crime is how you treated me! The Rangers couldn't even give me a proper laboratory."

"We have an operational budget," Qwark explained.

"You called me 'King of the Nerd Herd,'" Nefarious moaned.

"It was a term of endearment!" Qwark insisted.

"Day after day, I slaved away, creating all the weapons and devices that made you look like a hero," said Nefarious.

"But you're not a hero. You're not even a good villain! You're the galaxy's biggest joke."

"Maybe," Qwark said, clenching his jaw. "But now the last laugh . . . is on you." He aimed his blaster at Nefarious.

Nefarious squinted at him and held up a hand. "Wait . . . what? That didn't make any sense."

"Sure it did." Qwark grinned, still pointing his gun.

Nefarious shook his head. "No, it didn't. It sounded like you were combining 'the joke is on you' with 'I'll have the last laugh.'"

"Take your pick," Qwark shrugged.

"That's not how it works!" Dr. Nefarious screamed. "If you're going to use a one-liner, it should make sense and be relevant to the situation."

"Look," Qwark said diplomatically. "I workshop thousands of these a year and they can't all be gold. Now put your hands in the air!"

"Over *your* dead body!" Nefarious said. He aimed his blaster at Captain Qwark.

The final battle was on!

CHAPTER TWENTY

"GET READY TO ENGAGE MAG-BOOSTERS," Brax ordered through his communicator. The *Phoenix* and all the Rangers' Mag-Booster ships were nearing the top of the Deplanetizer. It was time to magnetize Drek's ship and pull it off course. Action!

"But Ratchet and Clank are still inside," Cora said.

"Drek's going to fire at Umbris at any moment," Brax argued. "We don't *have* any more time. Full power!"

The Rangers aimed their Mag-Boosters at the top antenna of the Deplanetizer. Slowly, the enormous weapon ship began to tilt.

Brax nudged the Mag-Boosters up to hyperdrive, and the station tilted further—a little more, and it would be pointing away from Umbris altogether!

"It's working!" Cora cheered. "Stay with it. Steady now!"

Inside the Deplanetizer, Qwark, Nefarious, Ratchet, and Clank were all being tossed around as the Rangers' Mag-Boosters pulled the enormous ship from side to side.

"What's happening?" Dr. Nefarious demanded.

"Deplanetizer now online," a computer droned nearby. Nefarious stepped up to the command console and grabbed a lever.

Ratchet was too far to stop him, but he screamed, "Qwark! Don't let him turn it on!"

Qwark grabbed for Nefarious's leg, trying to pull the evil doctor away from the controls. Nefarious shook him off. "Get off me, you has-been!" He kicked Qwark in the face, and then scrambled forward. He pounded his fist down on the POWER button, igniting the Deplanetizer.

As the lasers powered up, Nefarious grinned. "You know, maybe Drek was right. Maybe I *am* a mad scientist!"

Energy swirled out of the Deplanetizer's oculus. Light blasted from the core, shooting a powerful blast at Umbris. It blazed toward the volatile planet—narrowly missing contact.

"They missed!" Elaris cheered. Their Mag-Booster plan had worked!

The blast from the Deplanetizer soared through the galaxy, snaking its way toward a different target. Alone on New Quartu, Drek had just returned to his Blarg form. He brushed off his suit, fuming about how Nefarious had double-crossed him and turned him into a stinking sheep.

"That lousy, insolent, idiotic—" He broke off. Drek gazed up into the sky just in time to see a giant laser making its way right for him.

A moment later, New Quartu was nothing more than scattered pieces floating through the galaxy again—and Drek was no more.

The Deplanetizer was out of control. The inertia from its blast propelled the spaceship through the atmosphere. It was speeding toward the planet Umbris. In just a few minutes, the ship would crash and burn—and everyone inside would be smashed to smithereens.

"Ratchet," Elaris warned. "You have to get out of there!"

"Yeah," Ratchet said. "We're working on it."

Using his swingshot, Ratchet pulled himself and Clank up toward the command console. He had to save Captain Qwark!

As Ratchet raced toward his fellow Ranger, Nefarious squared off against Qwark. He was determined to have the last word.

"My plan! You've ruined my plan!" Nefarious waved his enormous blaster at Qwark. "You've had this one coming a long time, Qwark!" He aimed the weapon at Qwark and cackled. "Of all my brilliant creations, this weapon remains one of my favorites. Meet the RYNO!"

The enormous blaster roared to life, whirring and spinning. Nefarious pulled back the trigger.

At that moment, Ratchet shouted, "Hey—Nefarious!" He swung a wrench at Nefarious, knocking him over the good old-fashioned way: with force, strength, and good timing. The RYNO backfired against Nefarious's body, electrifying its owner.

Off balance, Nefarious stumbled. He plunged off the edge of the platform, careening through the air.

"Meet . . . the Omni wrench," Ratchet called after him.

Nefarious kept falling, his legs and arms flailing, until he reached the Deplanetizer's central core. His body began to melt, and then he disappeared into the bright light of the lasers.

"Warning," the Deplanetizer's computers blared. "Now entering Umbris atmosphere."

Ratchet reached out, pulling Qwark away from the ledge and back to safety.

"Any ideas?" Qwark said, looking desperately at Ratchet and Clank. They all knew they had to get out of there *now* or they were toast . . . just like Nefarious.

Clank's eyes fell on Drek's motorized scooter. It wouldn't get them far—but as far as he could tell, it was their only hope of getting anywhere. He and Ratchet jumped onto the back, and Qwark steered them through the Deplanetizer's corridors at breakneck speed.

"Come on, guys. Get out of there," Elaris cried through the communicators. "Come on!"

"They'll never make it out in time," Brax said, hoping he was wrong. "We've got to help!"

"It's too late," Cora said. "There's nothing we can do."

Ratchet, Clank, and Qwark weaved through the hallways.

"We must find one of Drek's teleporters!" Clank said.

"I saw one on the bridge," Qwark said, heading that way.

"Watch out!" Ratchet screamed. Pieces of the Deplanetizer were breaking away as the ship blasted through the atmosphere. Chunks of metal sailed toward them as they raced through the corridors.

"Hang on, boys," Qwark yelled, guiding them through the sliding doors that led out to the ship's bridge.

"It's here," Ratchet said, pointing at the round platform that could teleport them back to safety. "Hit the brakes!"

"Relax," Qwark said. "I know what I'm—"

Ratchet, Clank, and Qwark all screamed. They were going so fast that when Qwark hit the brakes, the scooter barely slowed down. All three slid toward the edge of the bridge.

Ratchet and Clank both skidded to a stop just in time to keep from falling . . . but Qwark wasn't as lucky. He flew off the edge of the platform and landed on the ship's glass window below.

"Oh dear," Clank said. Qwark was too far to jump back up, and they didn't have time to pull him to safety.

"I can't reach you in time," Qwark yelled out. "Just get out while you can!"

Clank turned and ran back toward the teleporter. "Hmm," he said. "I have an idea."

"Teleporter charging," the computer droned.

Ratchet turned and watched from the edge of the bridge as Clank bumped up against the teleporter pad, trying to lift it. "What are you doing?" he screamed over the noise.

"Improvising!" Clank told him.

Ratchet ran over to help. Together, they pushed and pried at the teleporter pad—until finally, the whole thing lifted free!

Ratchet and Clank sprinted toward the edge of the bridge with the teleporter. As one, they leaped off, sailing through the air as the Deplanetizer continued its descent toward Umbris. They only had a few seconds before the ship would crash land!

Ratchet and Clank clutched the teleporter as they

tumbled through empty space toward Captain Qwark. Qwark vaulted up, reaching for Ratchet's hand. Ratchet stretched out, his fingers clasping Captain Qwark's.

The Deplanetizer hit Umbris, the teleporter activated, and everything went white.

Moments later, Ratchet, Clank, and Qwark woke to find themselves sprawled out on the teleporter. Their eyes were clenched shut. Qwark gingerly opened his eyes and looked around. "Are we . . . are we dead?"

Ratchet sat up and looked around. Unless he was mistaken, they were back on the *Phoenix*!

"We are alive," Clank announced.

"All Rangers alive and accounted for," a computer voice sang out from somewhere nearby.

"Woo-hoo!" Elaris cheered through the communicator. "Welcome back, Rangers. Good job!"

Qwark rubbed his head, and then grinned sheepishly. "How many planets do you think I'll have to save before they call me a hero again?"

Ratchet shrugged, thinking about the advice Grim had given him. "You don't have to do big things to be a hero, Qwark. Just the right things."

Qwark smiled. Then he fished Ratchet's Captain Qwark trading card out of his pocket. He handed it back to Ratchet. "Who knows . . . maybe it will be worth something someday?"

Clank popped up between them. "I must say it is curious how the sudden cessation of velocity relative to our inertia did not cause either of you to—"

Ratchet keeled over and threw up. Loudly.

"Oh dear," Clank said.

"Don't worry, cadet," Captain Qwark said, patting Ratchet on the back fondly. "It happens to the best of— *hyunnngh!*" He bent over and vomited. "Oh . . . that was terrible." He ran from the room, stopping only to heave once more. "Make it stop!" he whimpered.

"Should we go and join the others?" Clank asked Ratchet.

"I'd like to," Ratchet said. "But first, there's a promise I have to keep to an old friend."

Clank nodded. "I understand."

"Don't worry," Ratchet told him. "I'm sure we'll run into each other again someday. It's a small galaxy."

"Well," Clank said, holding out his hand to shake. "I suppose this is good-bye."

Ratchet took his friend's hand in his own and shook. And shook. And shook some more. Eventually, Clank said, "You can let go now, Ratchet."

Then, with a final smile at his pal, Ratchet set out to fulfill his promise.

CHAPTER TWENTY-ONE

GRIM SHUFFLED THROUGH HIS REPAIR SHOP, grunting at the news reports that had been blasting out of the TV all day. He stopped, watching the Rangers' homecoming celebration unfold on the TV screen.

"That was the scene today," announced newscaster Dallas Wannamaker. "Thousands gathered to welcome home the Galactic Rangers, making their triumphant return from saving the galaxy. Grateful citizens gathered at the famed Hall of Heroes."

The television filled with images of the *Phoenix* landing and crowds surging forward to greet the heroes. The camera cut to a shot of Captain Qwark walking away from the *Phoenix.* "As for Captain Qwark, the recently demoted

Ranger will embark upon his galaxy-wide apology tour while shamelessly promoting his new book, *Listen, I Said I Was Sorry, All Right?*" Wannamaker continued. "When asked for a comment, the former Captain had this to offer . . ."

The camera focused on Qwark, who stared into the lens with intensity. "Prepare to be blown away by my epic humility."

The news story continued, flashing through images of Cora, Clank, Brax, and Elaris basking in the love of the adoring crowd. "There was, however, one curious absence from today's festivities. That of new Ranger sensation and media darling, Ratchet . . ." A picture of Ratchet flashed across the screen, and then the camera focused back in on Dallas Wannamaker. "Leaving this reporter with one question: What does a Lombax do after saving the galaxy? We may never know," the newscaster said solemnly.

Grim flicked off the TV, and then marched through his garage. Ships were lined up around the plateau, waiting for service. Finally, he had a technician help him get through the backlog of work!

"Come on, we haven't got all day! We have ten more proton scrubs to do before lunch if we want to stay on schedule!" he barked.

Ratchet popped out from under the ship he was busy working on. "I gotta be honest, Grim," he said. "I kinda thought you'd be so touched by the gesture of me coming back to help you out that you'd call us even . . ."

Grim smirked. "Well, you thought wrong, didn't you?" He pointed at the ship, urging Ratchet to get back to work.

Ratchet smiled, wiped his brow, and rolled back under the ship. A few minutes later, a voice called out, "Might I offer a suggestion?"

Ratchet rolled out from under the ship. He'd know that voice anywhere. It was Clank!

"Modifying that proton scrubber with a Gadgetron Quasar Flash would increase your efficiency by forty-seven point four percent," the little bot informed him.

Ratchet grinned at him. "A Quasar Flash, huh? Gee, I don't know. That kind of tech takes two to operate." He stood up and walked toward his pal. "And Grim's not as nimble as he used to be."

"Then perhaps I could remain here and assist." Clank picked up a bucket and some tools. "If you do not mind me staying around a while?"

"You kidding?" Ratchet said happily. "Things have been way too quiet without you around."

Clank tilted his head, considering. "I do bring a certain level of *zing* to the table, correct?" He chuckled.

Ratchet laughed along with him. "Yeah, Clank. You're a real wild one."

"Speaking of which," Clank said. "Am I to assume that you have retired from the Galactic Rangers?"

Ratchet smiled. "Nah. Once a Ranger, always a Ranger. Believe me, the minute somebody tries to blow up another planet, I'll be ready to go. But hey, what are the odds of that happening?"

"Precisely eighty-seven thousand, five hundred and thirty-four to one," Clank replied.

"Yup," Ratchet said, laughing again. "You're a real wild one, Clank."

Epilogue

ON THE EMPTY PLANET UMBRIS, a metal hand pushed through the smashed, tangled mess that was once the Deplanetizer.

Slowly, a form emerged from the rubble of destroyed ship. First, a green plastic skull with clockwork for brains poked out of the crash site. Then a pair of red eyes, glowing with hatred. Finally, a robotic body—saved from the ship's destruction by some miracle of science.

A new, improved Dr. Nefarious rose out of the rubble and ashes. Lightning sizzled in the sky as the mad scientist lifted his arms and cackled maniacally.

The doctor was back . . . and he was ready for more evil than ever!